Return to Eagle Cove

a small town Oregon romance

by

M. L. Buchman

Discover more by this author at:
www.mlbuchman.com

Cover images:
Walk Forest Couple © Leaf | Dreamstime.com
Douglas Fir Tree © Kongxinzhu | Dreamstime.com

Buchman Bookworks

Other works by M. L. Buchman:

Angelo's Hearth
Where Dreams are Born
Where Dreams Reside
Maria's Christmas Table
Where Dreams Unfold
Where Dreams Are Written

Delta Force
Target Engaged

Deities Anonymous
Cookbook from Hell: Reheated
Saviors 101

The Night Stalkers
The Night Is Mine
I Own the Dawn
Daniel's Christmas
Wait Until Dark
Frank's Independence Day
Peter's Christmas
Take Over at Midnight
Light Up the Night
Christmas at Steel Beach
Bring On the Dusk
Target of the Heart
Target Lock on Love
Christmas at Peleliu Cove
Zachary's Christmas
By Break of Day

Thrillers
Swap Out!
One Chef!
Two Chef!

SF/F Titles
Nara
Monk's Maze

Firehawks
Pure Heat
Wildfire at Dawn
Full Blaze
Wildfire at Larch Creek
Wildfire on the Skagit
Hot Point
Flash of Fire

Chapter 1

Friday Morning

Almost home, sweetie."

"Oh joy," Jessica Baxter tried to clamp down on her sarcasm. It was a bad habit that worked fine in her social set back in Chicago, but sounded more petty with each mile they drove toward the Oregon Coast. She slumped down in the passenger seat of her mom's baby-blue Toyota hybrid. It still had that new car smell. As much as she'd dreamed of owning a hot sports car some day, she knew that she was enough her mother's daughter that this was probably the exact sort of eminently sensible car she would buy when her VW Beetle finally gave up the ghost.

Just like her mom.

Maybe she'd get it in red to be at least a *little* different.

Jessica sighed again, keeping it to herself so that she wasn't being overly offensive. Her mother was one of the many reasons that she'd gone as far away as possible for college and did her best to rarely return—she didn't want to turn into her mother and it was too easy to imagine doing so if she'd stayed in the small town of Eagle Cove, Oregon.

They were like twins separated by twenty-two years. The two of them had been able to trade clothes since Jessica hit puberty and had shot up to match her mother's slender five-foot-ten. Other than a very brief mistake of dying her hair black as part of a tenth-grade dare, which had turned her fair complexion past goth and into bloodless vampire, they were both light blond.

The one part of twin-dom that she couldn't seem to pull off even though she wanted to was Mom's casual-chic. Monica Baxter was always dressed one step above the world around her; not fancy, just really well put together. The closest Jessica ever managed was Bohemian-chic which wasn't really the same thing, but she'd learned to make it her own. Of course, Bohemian was easier on the budget and often available in consignment stores which had only reinforced her chosen style.

Jessica did her best to not regress as they drove up into the Coast Range that separated the beach towns from the rest of Oregon…and failed miserably at that as well. She felt as if she was rapidly descending back toward being a pouty, pre-pubescent twelve from her present urban and worldly thirty-two.

Why did crossing the Oregon state line always take twenty years off her intelligence?

Maybe it was only Coast County. Because of the landscape the Oregon Coast felt incredibly far from anywhere. The Coast Range topped out at a mere four thousand feet high, but only a half dozen passes made it through the three hundred mile range of rugged hills that separated the beaches from the broad farming and industrial realm of the Willamette Valley. The interior of the state might as well be in a whole other country for how little it had in common with where she'd grown up.

"It's so strange being back here," Jessica rolled down the window and sniffed at the air. The scents were so rich and varied that they tickled. Bright with pine. Musty with undergrowth. Damp. A first hint of the sea.

"Well, it has been four years, honey. That's bound to make it seem a bit odd. But I'm so glad that you came."

"Me too, Mom." Better. She managed to say it as if she meant it, however unlikely that might be. Chicago fit her like a…but it didn't. The city was…something she was not going to give a single thought to for the next eight days. If she didn't fit there and she didn't want to fit in Eagle Cove, Oregon, then where did she belong?

Jessica breathed in deeply this time, trying to clear her thoughts with the fresh air of the Coast Range and nearly choked herself on how green everything smelled. The harsh slap of the mountains was almost an affront. The two-lane road dove and twisted along narrow corridors sliced through towering spruce and Douglas fir trees. The babies were sixty feet high along the shoulder as the car twisted up toward the pass; the mother trees behind them were much, much bigger.

And it wasn't just the trees that were lush. As they wound deeper into the Coast Range, each branch became covered with mosses and lichens. It soothed her eyes, so used to towering concrete and glass, with a living tapestry of greens, golds, and silvers. Beneath the trees grew an impenetrable tangle of salal and scrub alder. Old barns on the roadside didn't have shingle roofs, they had moss ones; some of them were covered inches thick. Many RVs, left unattended in front yards for too long, had a sheen of green growth on their north side.

"I really want to hate this," the Coast Range had three times the rainfall of Chicago, often surpassing a hundred inches a year. She expected to feel the weight of all that biomass crashing down on her shoulders, but instead she noticed the start of a disconcerting lightness as if coming home was a good thing. Jessica did *not* like that encroachment of pending appreciation, perhaps even enjoyment, upon her *true* feelings. "But it smells so good. Like sunshine and new growth."

Her mother's laugh was amused as they twisted along the two-lane road slowly climbing up a narrow valley.

"I didn't mean to say that out loud."

"But you said it anyway."

"Not helping, Mom."

Thankfully her mother's laugh said that she had understood Jessica's response as a tease. Which it mostly was, partly.

Jessica didn't *want* to like coming back to the coast. She didn't have small-town dreams. That was the main reason she'd left Eagle Cove. She had big city dreams…which weren't exactly coming together for her despite her efforts over the last fourteen years. But scurrying home wasn't going to fix those. And the selection of men in such a tiny town was, to put it kindly, pitiful. Puffin High—

Why they hadn't called it Eagle High in Eagle Cove was a subject of heated debate by every single class.

Puffin High's problem was that she knew every male her age all too well. The only reason the town had its own high school was that it was too far away from everywhere else for busing to make sense. Her senior class had just thirty-four students. Grades seven through twelve numbered under two hundred. And she knew far too much about every single one of them.

Even more obnoxiously invasive on her sense of right and wrong, instead of dumping rain, it was a perfect day. The sun sparkled down revealing a thousand shades of green in the living walls that lined the road. The air coming through the open window was thick with pine sap and the gentle tang of rotting undergrowth. There was so much oxygen in the air that it made her feel a little giddy.

Yes, a perfect day, if she'd been alone…and still in Chicago.

"I could have rented a car and saved you the drive, Mom." Actually, her budget had been thrilled when her mother had offered to come and fetch her. Also, once in Eagle Cove there wasn't a lot of use for a car, except when the rain poured down. The whole town was only a few miles long and she could walk most places she'd want to go. As if there were any old haunts that she'd care to revisit. She'd made good her escape to Northwestern University's School of Journalism at eighteen but every now and then the town still sucked her back.

"Nonsense, honey. I'm always glad to drive up and get you. Besides, I needed a few things for the wedding."

"How many is this?" As if she didn't know. It took much of her journalistic skill to keep "that judgmental tone" out of her voice. Something her early teachers had dinged her on until she'd learned to eradicate it. But since she was regressing as they neared the coast, it was trying to make a comeback.

"Number four."

"Why, Mom?"

"Because I love the man." Her mother actually glanced away from the road to offer her a scowl. "I'd have thought that was obvious."

"It is. But you've divorced him three times."

"Because *your* father can drive a woman bat-shit crazy without even trying." They giggled together because that was an absolute truth about Ralph Baxter.

"I meant, why marry him again? You're both legal age, your daughter lives in Chicago," and wouldn't complain if she lived on another planet entirely. "Just shack up together. Then you can lock the door whenever Daddy becomes too much like himself."

Ralph Baxter was always getting caught up in monster projects. Without a word of warning he would suddenly rip out the entire kitchen, once on the morning before a dinner party, because he'd thought of a better way to design it. Or he'd start building a new boat from scratch in the middle of the driveway, rather than in the generous side yard, which blocked parking near the house for months.

"Oh, honey. I'm too old fashioned a girl to 'just shack up.'"

Which was almost believable, even in the twenty-first century. To hear Aunt Gina—who despite her name was as not-Italian as a pastrami sandwich—tell it, Monica Lamont had chosen Ralph Baxter as her sweet sixteen love. She'd never even shopped around. How 1950s was that for a woman who hadn't even been born then?

Jessica had shopped plenty, or at least window-shopped. She'd found only a few men worth the cost of trying on for size. Definitely not a one worth taking home to keep. She might look like her mom, all blond, tall, and waiflike—which she kind of hated though the men seemed to like it—but inside she wanted to be like Aunt Gina.

Luigina Lamont looked nothing like her twin sister…or Grandpop…or much like Grandma for that matter. She was a statuesque redhead, in every voluptuous sense of the word and completely lived up to her name: Luigina meant "Famous Warrior." Her merry laugh slapped up against you at the most unexpected moments and constantly poked at your ticklish spot until you were curled up on the couch begging her to stop. Unlike Mom and her serial marriages to the same man, Gina brought home plenty yet had only tried to keep one.

That "unholy disaster" (as the family tales described it) had produced Natalya Daphne Lamont—Jessica's three-hour-older (and Natalya never let her forget it) first cousin and best friend. Just like Gina, Natalya didn't look like either her mom or Gina's brief husband. Maybe that was hereditary on that side of the family to balance out how much Jessica resembled her own mom and their shared grandma. Jessica had a sudden flash of her own future daughter looking just like her…and felt the world spin just a little at thinking about children at all.

"If I hadn't seen her come out between my legs myself," Aunt Gina would announce loudly, "I'd have thought I adopted the kid. Maybe I signed up to be a surrogate then forgot all about it."

Mom blushed every time Aunt Gina let that one loose in public, without understanding that if she didn't, Aunt Gina would have stopped long ago.

"Such an exotic offspring deserves an exotic name. Natalya for the Russian Bond girl in *GoldenEye* and Daphne for du Maurier the romance writer, not the nymph who had to turn into a tree to escape that lusty jerk Apollo." The fact that *GoldenEye* hadn't come out until Natalya had already been in grade school hadn't changed Aunt Gina's story one bit.

Maybe Jessica's own child would be lucky and take after Cousin Natalya who was slender like Jessica, but had all of the curves Jessica had prayed for throughout her teenage years but never been granted. Natya was also dusky skinned like a permanent tan and leggy like some French model. Jessica's and her mom's fairy light hair and Aunt Gina's mass of red curls had been transformed to a smooth cascade of dark chestnut on her cousin. Yet she and Jessica felt like twins from different mothers: one light, one dark, but much the same on the inside.

Jessica smiled at the sign as they cleared Maxine Pass: eight-hundred and three feet according to the sign. The "three" always made her laugh. It was like Becky, her other best friend from Eagle Cove, firmly insisting that she as five-four "and a quarter" as if it made a difference.

Maxine Pass was technically Maxwell Pass. Or it had been until the day that Aunt Gina had declared it just wasn't right for all of the passes to have male names merely because men were the ones who drew the maps back in the 1800s.

For her sixteenth birthday Jessica hadn't received her first kiss—already happened a year before—or gotten laid—two more years until that event. Instead, she'd been recruited for a "Mission!" At two in the morning on their shared birthday, Aunt Gina drove her and Natalya up to repaint the Maxwell Pass highway sign to Maxine. It had become a tradition that every time the highway department changed it back to Maxwell, the three of them would have a two a.m. gals' outing and change the sign once again. The highway department had given up years ago. A few of the more recent road maps had even changed the name.

"Girl Power!" they'd shout after each time they finished repainting the sign, usually about three a.m. Then they'd break out the thermos of hot chocolate and drink it from a shared cup while they admired their handiwork by moonlight.

One time Martin, the town cop, had shown up while they were doing it. Jessica and Natalya had ducked, but Gina hadn't slowed down a single brush stroke.

"Thought it would be you," Martin had observed through his open car window, obviously talking to Gina.

"Out of your jurisdiction, Marty," had been Aunt Gina's awesomely calm reply. She had always been Jessica's hero, but that totally clinched it. The town limits had been left far behind.

He'd joined them for the hot chocolate and had a good laugh at the "Girl Power!" chant.

Today Jessica just waved hello to the sign as they crested the pass and began their descent.

"Didn't you ever bust out, Mom?" Jessica tried to imagine her doing so, but couldn't quite conjure it up in her mind.

"Bust out? You mean cheat on your father? Never!"

"But what about between times, when you were divorced? That wouldn't be cheating."

Monica Lamont's lips thinned as she tightened her jaw and finally shook her head in a sharp little snap. "I was only living in the other end of the house."

"What about with Dad? You and Dad could just…you know?" The thought of her parents having sex was uncomfortable enough that she couldn't quite say it aloud.

"Ralph says that if I feel so strongly about things that I have to divorce him, then I shouldn't be expecting any special concessions while we are divorced."

Jessica felt she had to side with Dad on that one. He'd become used to his wife's antics, but that meant he didn't get any either in the interims. No wandering for him—it had always been clear that Ralph Baxter was absolutely crazy about Monica Lamont. Jessica felt kind of sorry for him.

"Wait. You mean you haven't had sex in two years?" This latest was their longest divorce yet.

Again that little snap that made Jessica's neck ache in sympathy. Mom moved to the right as the road added a climbing lane to reach the six-hundred and thirty-four foot (not quite so much bragging) Rogue Pass. That name at least made perfect sense by Oregon standards…because it wasn't anywhere near either of the two separate Rogue Rivers in Oregon. A half dozen cars roared past. Mom always drove exactly at the speed limit instead of the nearly mandatory ten over that prevailed throughout the state.

"So you're waiting for the wedding night?"

This time her mom's nod was a little sad.

"I'm sure tomorrow will be a great night, Mom."

At that she smiled brilliantly. "If the past three are anything to judge by, yes, it will be. It's just too bad we had to delay it."

"Delay it? Wait! What?" Jessica bolted upright in the car seat and almost throttled herself with her seatbelt. The wedding was supposed to be *tomorrow*. She'd secretly planned on staying just one day past the wedding, and then catching the Airporter Express that wandered through the small coastal towns once a day. She'd already warned Natalya to expect her in Portland for the rest of the week until her flight back to the Windy City.

"Well, we were meeting with Judge Slater about the ceremony. As he performed the first three weddings…"

Jessica resisted pointing out that he'd done all three divorces as well. Maybe her Oregon civility was coming back. Yeah, like a toothache.

"…and he had all of the old records in a file; even had the new marriage license pre-filled out, the dear man. However, it turns out that the first time we were married was on July fourteenth, not July seventh as I had remembered. You know how your father loves the cycle of things. So we moved the wedding to next weekend to coincide properly with the original. I knew you already had your plane tickets, so I didn't see any point in telling you."

Didn't see any point? She'd have moved heaven and earth to— Actually, her mother was right because she'd purchased the cheapest non-refundable, non-changeable tickets she could find.

A week! She was going to be trapped in Eagle Cove from Friday morning until Sunday morning nine days later? Oh, that was so bad.

"I can't believe that we celebrated it wrong for all of those years," her mother continued, completely oblivious to the panic she'd just created. "The seventh was the date that had always stuck in my head for our anniversaries."

Mom's dropping voice spoke volumes. She'd always been terrible at keeping a secret.

"So why *did* the seventh stick in your head?" Jessica kept it as casual as she could, rather than rubbing it in that her mom always gave up whatever she was trying to hide. It must be the journalist in her coming out: ask the question and then wait patiently for a reply. Not pushing was another change between them. Jessica didn't feel as if she was mellowing with age, but perhaps she was. Being disillusioned at thirty-two was no more newsworthy than it had been at twelve or twenty-two; but a woman shouldn't mellow until…well, maybe a hundred-and-two.

On the back side of Rogue Pass, Mom concentrated on the winding descent. Jessica waved at a massive Roosevelt elk who grazed in a small clearing beside the road. Coming back to Eagle Cove might be only one step better than a nightmare, but it was a very scenic one. The road was soon joined by a stream rushing in a deep ravine on Jessica's side of the road; the problem was that they were both racing in the wrong direction—toward, not away from, her childhood home. The stream tumbled along almost as fast as they did down toward Eagle River which would eventually define the end of town where it opened into a broad bay before it reached the sea.

No one quite knew why the bay had been named a cove, but it showed that way on even the oldest maps. It gave the town an off-kilter personality to Jessica's mind, as if it was always seeking to find its true identity. No bridge crossed the Eagle to the wilderness area on the other bank. To reach that required either a boat or an hour drive back up to Highway 101, across the river, and then a long crawl back to the Coast over marginal logging roads.

"C'mon, Mom, give." Since not pushing at her mother had failed, Jessica went with regressing and shifted to the wheedling tone she'd perfected as a child. She might hate herself in the morning for slipping back into it, but it always worked. Sure enough, her mom gave in right on cue.

"July seventh was the one time we cheated. We didn't actually wait for our first wedding night," the blush on her mother's fair skin was almost bright enough to lighten the dark corridor between the towering trees. "Your father made it amazing. But that's also the day I became pregnant, though I didn't know it until after the wedding. All those years I was celebrating the wrong date. That's why we never fool around unless we're married."

"Sounds like you were celebrating *exactly* the right date, Mom." She tried to pin down the exact date of her own first time, but it hadn't been all that memorable. Good, but "earth-shattering" was just another one of those 1950s' myths that didn't happen in the twenty-first century. Except, apparently, for her own mother. How unfair was that.

"Maybe," her mom admitted, "but we're going to get married on the fourteenth anyway."

"So, I'm a bastard?" Not that it bothered her, but she couldn't resist needling her mother about it. Maybe she hadn't matured all that much.

"Yes dear, but only by one week. I swear I didn't know." This time Jessica heard that her mom's confession was a sigh at Jessica's question rather than sounding contrite. Maybe it was time Jessica grew up a bit—even when in Eagle Cove.

"Does Aunt Gina know about all this?"

"No one does, except your father and now you. You only arrived three days early, which was actually four days late. No one gave it any thought."

Excellent! To hell with being mature. Aunt Gina would love the extra dirt for teasing her sister and Jessica couldn't wait to be the one to tickle her aunt's funny bone.

# # #

It had been another long morning of assisting the Judge—always with a capital J. Monday through Friday, six a.m. to ten, Greg Slater helped his father. At first it had been something that Greg did to help out, but he'd come to like the simple routines and structure to his mornings.

"Ready?" he called back to the kitchen as he did every day. There was no real need to ask. The big old clock hung high on the wall said it was exactly six a.m. and the Judge was a very punctual man.

But Greg looked for the solemn nod before moving out into the diner and flicking on the fluorescents, "The Puffin Diner" sign, and the porch lights. There wasn't much need for the last, sunrise was twenty minutes ago, but the sun itself wouldn't clear the Coast Range ridge until at least six-thirty. For now, Beach Way, the town's main street, was mostly cool shadows and darkened buildings.

The bell mounted on the back of the door rang almost right away as Cal Mason Jr. came in. Greg had already set a mug of coffee on the counter for him. Cal ran the Blackbird Bakery and was hours into his day. Five days a week he was as punctual as the Judge. Cal Sr. wouldn't be in for a few hours yet.

"Your standard, Cal?"

"Double," though Greg knew that was a joke. Cal was one of the few men in town big enough that he could have eaten two of the Judge's generous portions. Six-two and as powerful as a bulldozer; his hands dwarfed the coffee mug.

Because Cal sat at the six-stool wooden counter, the Judge was less than five feet away through the broad service window that connected the dining room with the kitchen, but he waited for Greg to fill out the order slip and clip it to the spinner.

It was Greg's own damn fault. The diner's service had been a bone of contention, or rather "lengthy negotiation" just as most things were with the Judge.

"They can pick up their own damn plates at the window. Coffee pot is right there behind the counter where anyone who wants a refill can get their own."

Greg had won that round by subterfuge. He'd numbered the tables and then only put the numbers on the order slips, making it impossible for the Judge to boom out with "Veronica, your order is up." Customers had slowly adapted to not having to leave their tables for every little thing.

At least Greg thought he'd won, until a full three weeks later his father had winked at him while sliding across a short stack with bacon and hash browns for Karen Thompson, "Like I don't know who orders what on a Thursday."

Now the Judge wouldn't cook a thing without a proper ticket. Well, he'd cook it, but he wouldn't serve it no matter how busy or harried Greg was.

Cal's plate came up less than thirty seconds after Greg hung the ticket just as it did every morning: western omelet, hash browns, farm sausage, and English muffin. The last was about the only kind of bread that Cal didn't bake.

"Gotta have something that I can order out for and enjoy without baking it myself."

Greg moved the plate across to the counter and refilled Cal's half-drained mug of coffee.

There wasn't much call for a judge in a town the size of Eagle Cove. Semi-retired for the last five years, he no longer spent three days a week in Newport to sit on the bench as he had throughout Greg's childhood. Instead he'd set up a small courtroom in town. He mainly handled family matters like marriages and estates, and fines for drunk and disorderly tourists who soon learned that Judge Slater was a fierce protector of the town. There was only the occasional speeding ticket—no matter how hard Martin the cop tried to catch someone. The town was perched against the Pacific Ocean at the dead end of a winding two-lane that had left the coastal highway a dozen miles back; it had enough "Sharp Curves Ahead" signs to quell even the most lead-footed of souls.

So, "for something to keep me busy," the Judge held office hours only in the afternoons because his weekday mornings were all spent working as a short-order cook. And ever since Greg's return to Eagle Cove three years ago, he'd been his father's front-of-house man: waiter, cashier, and busboy.

The Puffin Diner had been a near derelict before his dad had bought and reopened it. It was a classic small town place built to serve the early morning fishermen, especially those returning from a long night's work on the offshore shoals; it was little changed over the last ninety years.

The clapboard building stood high enough on a heavy stone foundation that even the Christmas storm flood of 1964 had crested two steps below the front entry. It was one of the only structures on the town's main street that didn't have a street-level entry. All of the other businesses that had existed then had high-water lines drawn halfway or more up their walls. The Grouse Hardware store, the lowest spot in town close beside the docks, had a small wooden plaque of a fish screwed in just above the main door lintel. It was bright yellow with "Dec 22, 1964" painted on it in tropical blue—it was generally considered to be a little boastful, but old man Jaspar refused to tone down the color scheme that he'd painted on that fish in his youth.

The interior of the diner was so retro that it would have been ironic-modern if it wasn't quite so authentic. The steel-edged tables of blue Formica were scuffed nearly colorless by the thousands of plates and silverware settings that had been slid across their surfaces over the years. The chairs' red leather was sun-faded and the old chrome had pitted with rust from the salt air, making them uncomfortable to the touch without quite being painful. The linoleum floor had been replaced…back in the 1980s when mauve and hunter green had been trendy colors. The six round stools bolted to the floor at the counter squealed every time someone spun on or off them. The kitchen was authentic right down to the large service window, the steel spinner rack for order slips dangling in one corner, and the big grill and burners in the back. The scents of eggs, hash browns, and frying bacon filled the main street each morning enticing all passersby to come and find comfort food.

Ralph Baxter and Manny McCall came in and took their usual spot by the corner window. They'd have tourists out fishing off their boats within the hour and were both after black coffee and tall stacks.

At first Greg had resented serving the Judge's fare—it was as invariable as his father. Scrambles, omelets, pancakes—no waffles because the iron had broken the same day Mom had died and he couldn't seem to fix it and wouldn't let Greg try. The pancakes were big and fluffy. The very crispy hash browns were not an option; they were on every single plate, even with the pancakes. Farm fresh sausage or bacon was the other staple on every plate—not that it was a choice. Everyone received whichever Carl Parker had delivered the day before along with the eggs.

All of Greg's efforts to vary the oatmeal recipe, served with bacon or sausage and hash browns of course, had been in vain. The Judge served only rolled oats—not steel cut—with sliced, not diced, dried apricots and diced, not sliced, fresh apple. Whether brown sugar or maple syrup was used to sweeten it was wholly up to the customer; local honey was also available.

Omelets were the Judge's real specialty and by six-thirty there were already a dozen slips up for them. Omelets were the only dish where variations were allowed. He offered them with cheese, mushrooms, or smoked salmon fillings. Never all three of course, because there were limits to what was proper.

The Puffin Diner mostly served coffee. Greg's sole triumph at adjusting the menu had been when he managed to switch from Dad's "fresh ground" granules purchased in large plastic tubs to fresh-ground French roast. Tea or hot chocolate were the only other options, but asking for marshmallows with the latter was frowned upon unless you were a kid—the whipped cream came out of a spray can.

They'd fought royally over the Judge's inflexibility, but of course fighting over things was a tradition in the Slater household. Not that voices were ever raised, because that would never do. The few times Greg had tried that tactic he'd been ruled "Out of Order" and banished from the dinner table: the sole forum for Slater "discussions." With Ma gone to cancer three years before—Greg's original reason for returning to Eagle Cove—he didn't have the heart to "force" the Judge into driving him from the table after that first time. When he'd been remanded to the kitchen two weeks after Mom's funeral, he'd made the mistake of glancing back as he'd moved off to finish his meal. His father had looked old, sad, and impossibly alone.

Greg hadn't been able to face living in the big old house out on the beach, so he'd moved into the guest house. Once he finally understood that no number of cogent debates were going to sway the Judge, Greg had let the menu go. It had been unchanged in either content or price in the last decade—other than the wavy black line of magic marker through the "Waffles (with blueberries when in season)."

Greg had been on the verge of leaving town when the Judge sat him down at the big house's dining room table. Ma Slater had been in the ground for a month. Greg knew he didn't really have anywhere to go, he'd learned all he was going to from the banquet chef at the Sorrento Hotel in Seattle and there weren't any top positions open for an untested executive chef wanting to make his mark. He didn't have the capital to make his own splash, not in the insanely competitive restaurant markets in the big cities. But he'd find something.

"Been watching you, son. Been tasting your food," the Judge had tapped a fork on his dinner plate. Greg had roasted a pair of fresh-caught trout in hazelnut butter with a dressing of spring greens and homemade basil vinegar. Though Greg had cooked half the meals since Ma's funeral—"fair is fair" the Judge had declared—it was the first time his father had spoken of it.

"Uh-huh," Greg had gone for a neutral acknowledgement. He knew the Judge hated such prevarications, but Greg didn't know where this was heading and went for caution.

"This is good. Damn good."

Greg hadn't been able to offer even a neutral grunt over his surprise at the Judge's remark.

"Still needs some work, though."

Before Greg could snap at him about what did a man who scrambled eggs and ruled on law know about fine cuisine, the Judge continued.

"You need more seasoning," and he aimed a fork at Greg's chest, "and I'm not talking about salt. Your technique is the best I've ever seen, but I don't taste anything special. There's nothing here that isn't in any other fine restaurant. You need time to find your own voice, not some other chef's."

"My own voice?" But he didn't need to ask, he'd heard it a thousand times growing up.

The Judge looked down at the trout, one of the only times he'd ever said anything without looking at whoever he was addressing straight in the eye, "Your mother taught me that."

Ma had been a painter, a good one. Her seascapes had sold in galleries up and down the coast. Tillamook, Newport, Gold Beach, they all snapped up as much as she could produce and was willing to let go of—Grosbeak Gallery in town had always gotten first pick though. She'd often talked about finding your voice in your art so that it didn't look like everyone else's.

"So, here is the deal I'm offering you."

Greg knew that it wouldn't be open to negotiation; no one negotiated one of Judge Slater's "deals."

"The diner is mine on weekdays from six to ten every morning. I'd like you to stay as my assistant because you're good at it. That pays rent here at the house, a small salary, and we split the tips. What you do with the diner for the rest of the time, that's up to you."

And for three years, Greg had stayed in Eagle Cove and searched for his own voice. In the first year, he'd never cooked for anyone but himself and his father—who never again spoke about the food itself. Then one night Greg had invited a couple of buddies from high school who were still in town to the diner, as a test audience. Word got out about how good it was and folks had started asking when he'd do it again.

He'd eventually started "Irregular Friday Dinners at The Puffin." He only opened when he had a new meal to test. It was all *prix fixe,* fixed price—a twenty in the jar—and a set menu. After two years of those he felt almost ready to take his cooking out into the world; maybe spend a while as a pop-up restaurant—there and gone—rather than a full launch. He'd been saving his half of every morning tip and every goddamned cent for when he went back to the cities. At first he'd simply been trying to be better by the time he left Eagle Cove, but he'd become obsessed with finding and perfecting his "chef's voice." He wanted it to be so clear that it was undeniable. When he went back to Seattle, no one would label him the protégé of Charlene at Maximilien's or Angelo at The Tuscan Hearth. He'd be his own—

The old brass bell screwed into the top of the diner's front door rang like a small ship was coming into port. Morning service peaked as usual around eight and had now tapered off to just a few lingering diners.

Greg glanced at the big-face clock which hung above the cash register—9:57—and suppressed a groan. Judge's rule was that if you were in the door by ten, you could take as long as you wanted. If it was ten sharp plus a second, you were turned away—"Fair is fair." Maybe they'd be quick; he'd had an idea for a savory roulade that he wanted to try out.

Greg turned back and had to blink, then blink again. The morning sunlight shone through the front window and silhouetted two dazzling blondes, their hair practically set afire by the sunlight streaming in from behind them.

Then his eyes adapted as they moved farther into the room.

Mrs. Baxter who was soon to be Mrs. Baxter once again.

And a woman he hadn't seen since the day she'd left for college, but he'd know anywhere.

Jessica matched his own five-ten and her hair, instead of being the waist-long waterfall he'd remembered, now floated about her shoulders in choppy wisps that framed a face of high cheekbones, full lips, and eyes that sparkled with mischief.

Halfway across the old linoleum floor, she stopped and looked at him.

"Greggie's gaping, Mom."

And he couldn't do a thing about it.

# # #

"He is, dear," her mother replied cheerily.

"Does he do that to you a lot?" It was starting to get unnerving. In very short order, it would start pissing Jessica off. He'd been three years behind her in school. She'd dated his older brother for a while—he's the one who earned her first kiss at fifteen, but not all that much more. Her prior visits home hadn't overlapped with either brother being here, though she'd eaten the Judge's breakfasts before and had been looking forward to some comfort food since they'd turned west across the Willamette Valley. Her lemon-curd brownie from Loretta's in Chicago was many hours behind and much too far away.

"I don't think he's doing it to me, Jessica."

"Well, it had better be us and not just me. We are two fairly dazzling women after all. Besides, if he does it much longer, he's likely to get a dinner plate cracked over his skull."

Greg Slater shook himself like a wet dog and replaced his gape with a cautious smile. He'd done a lot of growing up since she'd last seen him. The gangly kid—who'd spent large portions of his freshman year in the principal's office—had turned into such a decent-looking guy that she might not have recognized him if they'd passed on the street.

"Hi, Jess."

"Jessica." Her high school nickname was one of the things she'd left behind along with Eagle Cove. She and Jessie Hamilton had been in a lot of classes together and everyone had called them both Jess despite their opposing genders. "I'm not a man, so don't expect me to answer to a male nickname."

"No you're definitely not—" she could see where his eyes were going, along with his smile. She gave him a second to recover, then two. She didn't give him three.

Jessica picked up a dirty plate from a freshly vacated table. It had a pool of syrup and a large splotch of leftover ketchup on some crispy hash browns. With a quick grab, she captured both the front of Greg's apron and his belt—maybe his underwear as well but she wasn't going to think about that. She tipped the plate into the space over his flat abs and managed to shove it half down his pants for good measure.

Jessica ignored his squawk of protest, letting go as he back-pedaled away and almost landed on Cal Mason Sr.'s lap right in the middle of eating his tall stack.

"Let's sit over there, Mom," she waved hello at the Judge before they sat down. He flapped a spatula back in her direction.

The Judge never whispered, so she and the half dozen other late morning diners could hear him clearly when he told Greg, "Lady's got your number but good, son."

Did she ever.

Greg had been a real slouch, the classic underachieving little brother. A decade and a half later and he was still in town working as a waiter for his dad. He'd grown up lean and dark. His neat black hair hung to his collar and the close-cropped beard accented a strong chin. He'd have looked Keanu Reeves' dangerous if it wasn't for the easy smile that still hadn't quite gone away. Greg Slater had come a long way from being fifteen…other than being another Eagle Cove failure-to-launch kid.

The last time she'd seen him, he'd been just starting his sophomore year in high school and panting after Dawn something—the hussy of the class. They probably had a trailer down at the end of Shearwater Lane that was slowly returning back into forest in a state of semi-decay, with a half dozen little Greggies bouncing about.

Maybe she should track down Greg's big brother Harry when she returned to the real world. Last she'd heard he was still single and practicing law in New Orleans…not that she was that interested in living in New Orleans, but it was a great place to visit. Maybe have some fun while she was there. She could even set up a few interviews in the jazz clubs and then write off the trip as well as selling a couple of articles to the trades. A couple of human interest stories, maybe find something unique enough to turn into a feature as well.

Though that was getting harder and harder. A few years ago she'd been able to get an article by the *Rolling Stone Magazine* editor way more than twice a year. And AAA used to give her bimonthly space in their magazines, but that had dried up as well. The collapse of print journalism was finally catching up with her.

Maybe if she'd been a straight newsie, she'd have stood a chance, but she wasn't. She'd always enjoyed the special interest story. Someone or some place that had found a way to be exceptional. A hot band, an innovative inventor, an amazing kid…those were the stories that had fascinated her. They'd shaped her career. And now they were "fringe" stories that didn't command much share in the shrinking print journalism bucket.

E-magazines were worse, paying crap. The *Huffington Post* had offered her a regular blog column, for no pay at all, which said too much about the state of that part of the industry. Maybe she should do a piece on The Puffin Diner; there was a laugh. That was probably below even *HuffPo's* standards.

"So…" she took a deep breath and decided that since she didn't have a choice about being in town for the whole week that she'd agreed to come for anyway, she might as well put a good face on it. It wasn't like the editors of the world were in a bidding war for her next story.

She and her mother settled at a clean table beneath a watercolor painting of The Puffin Diner, one of Ma Slater's last, based on the date. "Not for Sale" was in bold type on the little card taped to the wall close beside the frame.

"So, tell me about the dress, Mom."

# # #

Greg retreated. Hell, he didn't retreat, he ran away. The old Monty Python gag about "That's one nasty rabbit" came too easily to mind. Jessica Baxter was beautiful and looked all sweet and…fluffy.

Then she shoved a plate of cold food down his pants, ramming it right down inside his underwear in front of everyone. Cal Sr.'s howl of laughter had followed him right back through the service door into the side hall.

The one bathroom was occupied, so he detoured through the service door into the kitchen, his only other option.

Judge Baxter kept tending his omelets, "temperamental things omelets, can't look away from them for a second." But Greg also knew from experience that the Judge missed nothing of what happened in his restaurant.

With nowhere else to go, Greg moved over by the clean-up sink and shed the apron and his pants. At least his underwear had caught most of it. He shed those, wiped himself down with a couple of wet paper towels and pulled his pants back on commando. Greg wasn't really a commando sort of guy.

His shirt had taken the brunt of the attack. He stripped it off over his head and chucked it into the laundry bag along with his underwear and yesterday's service apron. He crossed to where he kept a spare shirt on one of the dry good storage shelves, but had never thought to keep underwear there as well. Greg yanked on the fresh shirt and buttoned it up.

"Not a word," he muttered at the Judge as he wound a fresh apron about his waist.

"The court will maintain a respectful silence at this time," the old man said with a tone as dry as week-old toast.

Restored to some semblance of order, Greg returned to the dining area. Cal Sr. gave him a smile he wished he hadn't seen. "Don't know what you did to piss her off, boy, but you did it good."

Greg considered telling Cal a thing or two, except he and the Judge had been friends since before Greg was born, and Greg knew that was dangerous ground.

Plastering on his best *maître d's* smile, he grabbed two menus and returned to the Baxters' table. Yes. That was a safer way to think of it. Not Jessica's; the Baxters'.

"Good morning. Welcome back to town, Jessica."

If she had any remorse for her abrupt action, she wasn't showing it in the least. "Thanks, Greg," she took the one-sheet menu and turned to study it without saying anything else. He'd swear there was a laugh lurking somewhere below the surface, but with her face turned down, he couldn't see it.

"Can I get you anything to drink?" He already knew Mrs. Baxter's preference for black teas before noon and herbals after lunch and had brought that to the table with the menus.

"Hot chocolate. No whip. With marshmallows if you have them."

"What? Are you a child?" And Greg could have shot himself. The Judge's crazy rules about what people should and shouldn't want had ruined his brain.

Jessica looked up at him with steady eyes the light blue of an ocean wave with the sunlight shining through…just before it crested and broke, smashing the unsuspecting rocks.

"No," her look was very cool, but her tone had a laugh hidden in it somewhere. "Are you?"

"Am I what?"

"A child? Still twelve maybe?" The last added with a wry smile.

Greg opened his mouth, saw Mrs. Baxter's widening eyes—perhaps at the danger zone he'd just flown into. A quick glance to the side revealed that the Judge was watching him intently.

"Um, that would be no. I'm not still twelve. Nor thirteen."

"Fourteen then?" Jessica's smile lit her face, as if bantering with him was the best part of her morning. This wasn't Jessica Baxter of eighteen. He was now facing a formidable woman who absolutely knew that she'd totally unnerved him.

"Not fourteen either," was the best rejoinder he could come up with. Before he could lose even more ground he said, "I'll get your cocoa," and turned for the wait station. Greg did his best to ignore his father's courtroom stare—the one he used when the defense counsel was making a particularly specious argument fabricated from too many Internet searches.

"Chicken!" Jessica whispered just loud enough for him to hear. "Buck-buck-bu-caw!"

Then she and her mother broke into a flurry of giggles that he did his best to ignore.

Cal Mason, who'd been leaning over to hear the exchange, added another of his loud guffaws.

# # #

Jessica listened and made appropriate sounds in the right places about this time's wedding dress.

But she was having trouble focusing. The last time she'd seen Greg Slater he'd been a pimply underclassman. When she'd been dumping the plate's contents down his shorts, she'd found a flat stomach with no give. He was now a handsome man awesomely in shape.

That was a point that had been emphasized when he'd stripped off his shirt. She could only see him from the midriff up over the edge of the steel service shelf that separated the dining room from the kitchen, but Greg clearly worked out and, loser or not, it looked very good on him. She wasn't that shallow, not really. But she was less certain about how shallow her Coast County regression might ultimately make her.

When he delivered her hot chocolate, with the marshmallows, she kept her head down and pretended she was paying more attention to her mother than she actually was. He was nothing more than a Puffling—a baby puffin being the lamest sports mascot on the coast if you didn't count the UC Santa Cruz Banana Slugs. Greg might be a Puffling who hadn't had the skills or drive to get out of town, but he was a very attractive one. That utterly shallow part of her double-checked for the ring or a tan line as he set down the cocoa. Nothing. Didn't mean he wasn't—she'd learned the hard way—but it didn't mean he was either.

Not that she could possibly care.

Nine days and she'd be gone again, Friday through next Sunday.

A glance out the window showed that day one was almost half done already which she'd count as a good omen. The sun was almost due south, lighting the length of Beach Way brightly. She could see Cal Jr.'s beat up red pickup parked right next to Cal Sr.'s beat up blue pickup alongside the Blackbird Bakery. By the speed the people on the street were moving, they were locals running errands. They moved much slower than a Chicagoan but with purpose—like crows walking over to see if something was edible. The few tourists who were checking out the taffy and kitsch shops moved slower but with a frenetic energy—like sparrows never quite coming to roost.

Eight and a half days to go. It wasn't enough time for anything to happen, even if she was interested. Flings had stopped working for her before she got out of college. Since then it had become a slightly depressing quest for what she was starting to fear she'd never find, someone who loved her the way that her dad loved Mom.

She'd make sure to hit Cal's bakery while she was here. And see if Maybelle had any particularly good used books in Early Bird Books. At least one lunch at the Plover Bay Inn… Jessica turned away from the street with the sad realization that she could do everything she wanted to in the town in about a day and she still had eight to go.

Greg kept his fifteen-year-old thoughts to himself as he served them a pair of the fluffiest mushroom omelets available anywhere. She turned to nod her thanks to the Judge—he didn't cook fancy fare, but it was always the very best.

She also noticed that the Judge hadn't missed a single jot of his son's shortcomings. She'd always liked Harry and Greg's dad, but she wasn't so sure that she liked the look in his eyes at the moment. Jessica had learned the day after her first kiss with Harry that she could read Judge Slater's facial expressions *far* too easily, even if everyone else in town declared him to be wholly inscrutable. It was a skill that had served her well in journalism, too. She'd always been able to tell exactly what topic the interviewee was doing their best to avoid.

However, right now the Judge was looking at her as if he was having an idea that he found both interesting and curious. The last shift in his expression surprised her, partly because it was clear enough that anyone except a dunderhead like Greg would be able to see it.

Judge Slater had just decided that whatever he was thinking was pretty damned funny and that worried Jessica.

Not much amused the Judge.

# # #

Greg kept to the shadows after locking the door behind the last customers. It was almost eleven; the Baxters had taken their time. Jessica and Monica Baxter walked across Beach Way. Except Jessica didn't walk. She…

He wasn't sure what she did, but it was doing strange things to his thoughts.

Her sudden reappearance had hit him as hard as any slap—and he'd earned a few before he'd learned decent manners while still a high school sophomore. Seeing her so out of the blue took him back to when he was in seventh-grade and she was already an over tall and impossibly sophisticated fifteen; even then she'd had an amazing sense of style that set her apart from all of the other girls. That was the age when he'd started thinking that girls weren't just different than boys, but that the differences were very interesting.

Today she wore light slacks and a blouse that looked loudly… Hungarian, though he had no idea what a Hungarian blouse might actually look like. Perhaps it was the blue scarf loosely knotted about one wrist that made her look a bit like a blond gypsy.

Half of the fights he and Harry had as kids, and there'd been plenty, didn't have a thing to do with being brothers. Though he'd forgotten the reasons until this moment.

He'd seen Harry kiss Jessica Baxter, and a need to pummel his brother had burned to life inside him. They'd battled often enough over the next three years before Harry went to college for Greg to completely forget the reason behind it. Even after he'd grown up enough to stop getting into fistfights with his own blood-kin—an offense the Judge had curiously left completely for them to work out—Greg had never been able to explain why he'd begun in the first place. By the time he and Harry had discovered that they actually liked each other, about the same time Greg graduated from the Culinary Institute of America, Greg hadn't remembered the Jessica-based origin.

He did now…and felt incredibly stupid. He'd have to apologize to Harry the next time they talked. Jealousy, deep and dark green as the Coast Range forest. Impressively stupid, even on his personal, deeply sad scale of stupidity.

Out the window, Jessica slid into the far side of her mother's blue Toyota hybrid. Just before her face disappeared below the roofline, she looked back toward the diner. No—she looked right at him. Without noticing, he'd moved up to the diner's front window until his nose was practically pressed against the glass between the black-and-gold "e" and "C" in "Eagle Cove."

He could feel her laugh like a blow to his chest even if he couldn't hear it through the glass. Her sparkling laugh had him retreating once more into the shadows.

When he turned, his father was watching him watch Jessica, the grill's wire brush clenched in one yellow-gloved fist and a large sponge in the other.

"What?"

The Judge offered one of his thin, unreadable smiles.

"What?" Greg was sufficiently aggravated with himself for getting caught staring that the word came out loud and sharp. He half expected to be banished from the room.

Instead his father simply raised his eyebrows in mock surprise and said softly, "You always did have a soft spot for that girl." Then he turned back to cleaning the grill.

Greg didn't have a "soft spot" for Jessica Baxter.

She'd been his first mad crush and just now he'd learned that he'd never gotten over it.

Chapter 2

Friday Afternoon

It had been almost a decade since the previous wedding between her parents, and four years since Jessica's last visit to Eagle Cove. Her life had kept her busy and the time had slipped by too easily to notice.

To push back the guilt, she concentrated on the view out the car window as they drove through town.

It was amazing how little yet how much Eagle Cove had changed. Or rather how little it had changed and how much she noticed each detail that had. The Flicker movie theater across from the diner still had a massive chainsaw carving of a northern flicker woodpecker clutching the marquee, but it also sported a fading sign which proudly declared: "Now in Digital!" They were running *The Big Year*. She'd bet that they reran the birding film every year for the summer tourists coming to Eagle Cove for fair weather coastal birding. They'd probably bring it back in the spring too.

Grouse Hardware still had a pile of wheelbarrows stacked up out front that might be the same stack old man Jasper had rolled out there each morning since she could remember, but they also had a riding lawnmower parked in the next-to-the-door place of pride. She tried to think who in town had a big enough spread to justify a riding mower—coastal lots tended to be small and grass rarely thrived in the heavily salted wind. Then she realized that the town was growing older. The Judge's hair had mostly gone silver. Cal Mason Sr., in the diner eating his tall stack, was even rounder and balder than before. Maybe there was more demand for things like riding lawnmowers.

Jessica glanced worriedly at her mom, but she looked the same. Some lines around the eyes and mouth, but they made her look like she smiled more rather than less which Jessica knew to be true. With her good eye for clothes, and her automatic slap that dropped her cell phone into the hands-free mount every time they got in the car, Mom definitely looked in charge. However, Jessica's journalistic eye didn't miss that even in July, Eagle Cove Real Estate wasn't too busy for her to run up to Portland to fetch her errant daughter.

Mom wore her hair shorter than she had a decade ago, a neat, chin-long cut that looked good enough on her that Jessica might have to try it next time she cut her own hair. Of course Jessica also wore her own hair shorter than a decade before, so maybe that change didn't count for much.

The center of town stretched six blocks from the docks to the Rusty Pelican, the town's dive bar in both senses of the word. The Pelican looked even more disreputable than usual. Alistair Thomlinson had clearly found even more crap. An import from Cornwall, he was fascinated by "beach décor" beyond even cliché. The tired porched was curtained by a line of battered fisherman floats hanging from a beam. Old crabbing pots, a mostly deflated rubber raft, fishing poles, and chunks of driftwood added to the look. His *pièce de résistance* had always given Jessica the creeps. It was an old style dive suit with the sagging rubber body and the bulbous helmet now rusting in the coastal air.

Maybe she was okay with not being here so much.

Mom and Dad had taken to visiting her for the week between Christmas and New Years wherever she was—decreasing her need to come back. The first year in Chicago had been so bitterly cold, that they'd sworn a family pact to never make that mistake again. Washington, D.C. had been a little better the following year.

Since then they'd met in different, warmer locales until it had become their new tradition, working right across the bottom of the country: Key West, New Orleans, Austin, Phoenix, and a hilarious holiday at Disneyland and Universal Studios. The fact that Mom and Dad were divorced for that one hadn't diminished the fun in the least.

The first divorce had shocked a nine-year old girl to her very soul. Family was supposed to be forever. She knew because both her mother and her father had told her so. Mom hadn't gone far. At all. She'd moved through their home's breezeway into the mother-in-law unit that Granny Lamont had never occupied—she'd fallen for a Costa Rican millionaire and called herself his eighty-year old, bikini-clad squeeze. Her Christmas cards were invariably just that, the two of them on a gorgeous tropical beach in skimpy enough attire that the main thing they were each wearing was smiles.

Her mother, in staking her claim to the mother-in-law unit, had taped the divorce decree to the glass door that connected the two parts of the house. That first decree had been covered over with a marriage license after less than six months.

Jessica had been less shocked when the second decree covered over that in her junior year. Their shortest of the three divorces, the piece of paper that covered it was dated less than three months later. When her mother had declared she was done with him but good on Jessica's thirtieth birthday, Jessica had asked just one key question.

"Where did you put this time's divorce decree?"

"Why right over the top of that godforsaken third wedding license. I don't know what I was thinking when I remarried that man." The fact that it had lasted thirteen years this time and she hadn't moved *completely* out of the house since the day she'd moved in thirty years before was so irrelevant that Jessica didn't even bother to comment on it. Someday she'd find a man, housebreak him, and move in with him. Not a chance was she going to go to all the waste of doing paperwork to keep him.

Jessica's decision not to worry had been reinforced by the fun family vacation in southern California as well as when the three of them had made plans for Hawaii this next winter. They were already joking that Fiji would be the next stop after that, though Mom had temporized with maybe spending a Christmas at each Hawaiian island before going so far afield. It was just as well, Jessica's vacation fund wasn't likely to reach even to Hawaii.

But she wasn't going to think about that.

Past Jane's Warbler Market, her Mom turned onto LBB Lane.

"Your father has a group of tourists out on the boat fishing for the day—you might recall that it's inshore halibut season. He promised to try and be back in time for dinner. Meanwhile, I thought we'd get you settled in at Gina's." Jessica's old bedroom, with her blessing, had long since been turned into her mother's fitness room.

LBB Lane had always been one of Jessica's favorites. The town had been platted by a mother-daughter team. *The Book(let) History of Eagle Cove*—actually a double-sided tri-fold sheet of letter-sized paper run off on the Town Hall copier but bearing a grandiose title—listed them as amateur ornithologists. As if there'd been so many "professional" opportunities for women in an 1890s coastal fishing village.

What the brochure didn't say, though the local scuttlebutt definitely did, was that mother and daughter couldn't stand each other. So they'd divided the town in half. Everything toward the ocean from Beach Way had been decreed for Mother Mason to lay out, which she'd done with the names of all of her favorite land birds. In retaliation Daughter Mason had chosen seabird species for everything in her control, from Beach Way to the forest. Unwilling to risk the ire of either, who were apparently both elemental forces, store owners cautiously named their businesses for which side of the main street they were on. Land bird businesses stood on the ocean's side of Beach Way and seabird-named ones roosted on the side toward the forest.

But a dozen streets on either side of Beach Way were all that would fit between the sea and the narrowing of the river valley back up toward the pass. Mother Mason, in a fit of despair at not being able to include so many of her favorites, had made the last road LBB Lane. Little Brown Bird Lane covered finches, wrens, tits, juncos, and a whole gamut of others even if the proper name wouldn't fit on a street sign. The lane had been extended with time until it become the longest street in town. It ducked down close to the sandy beach before climbing south and up on top of the basalt cliffs. A straggling, graveled one-lane finally ended at the long-since automated and incongruously named Orca Head lighthouse.

Jessica had somehow forgotten how breathtakingly beautiful the beach and cliffs were, though they were the least changed of anything in Eagle Cove. Just a block off Beach Way, LBB Lane took a sharp left turn to the south and ran along a bank that stood a dozen feet above an amazing stretch of sand. No Florida or California beach could compare. Those were tamed, crowded with condos, or fenced away in tiny sections for rich people's personal enjoyment.

Almost the entire Oregon Coast had been grabbed for the state by Governor Oswald West back in the early 1900s. It had ruined his political career; but it had also guaranteed that the beach would remain unspoiled and accessible to all. There was a wildness to it that she'd never seen anywhere else.

"Stop! Mom, stop the car. I have to—" she didn't know quite what came over her. She was wrestling the door open even before the car was fully stopped.

In panic, Mom stomped on the brakes and the door nearly slammed forward out of Jessica's grasp.

"Sorry, I just—" Jessica tried to apologize as she jerked her seatbelt free. Out of the car, she clambered down the bank over the big rocks and a couple of driftwood giants that some massive storm had cast up high on the beach. The former were scrubbed clean by hard wave action and the latter were dark brown, stripped of their bark by the same relentless pounding of the waves that eventually had delivered them.

The beach south of the Eagle River's outlet was a stretch of feldspar buff-yellow sand with streaks of darker iron from the erosion of the basalt cliffs to the south. At low tide, like it was now, the beach was fifty yards wide and a couple of miles long. High tide would shrink it to ten yards and chop it into three or four sections—depending on the height of the tide—divided by rocky headlands that stretched out from the shore.

She shed her sandals and dug her toes down into the cool sand. Even on a sunny day, the sand was rarely hot along the coast. And a few inches down, a layer of cool dampness eased it even further. The waves were small today. Rollers of just three to five feet fell on the beach with a deep-throated sigh of relief. Having traveled across thousands of miles of ocean from Alaska, Japan, or Hawaii, they had reached their goal and arrived with a thump of joy and a sand-slapping high five of a job well done.

Jessica closed her eyes to the bright sun glinting off the white of the breaking curls and simply breathed in. The air, cleansed by a hundred storms as it crossed the wide Pacific, tickled her hair about her neck. Gulls nattered as they debated whether it was time to walk the beach as dignified as stout old men waddling off to the pub or should they fly out past the waves to ride the gentle swells up and down through the pleasant afternoon. Any sounds made by the tourists on the beach were whisked away before they reached her.

"I don't think I've ever seen you so affected by the ocean," her mother spoke from close beside her.

"I—" Jessica didn't know what to say. It wasn't that she'd missed the ocean. She'd been at a conference in St. Petersburg just two months back, but it hadn't felt like this. Her reactions were backward anyway. St. Pete's had bath-warm water and languid waves that lapped a few inches higher when it was high tide; a thoroughly enjoyable place to lounge and swim.

The Oregon beach was all about character, tough character—often as not it tried to kill you. The water driven by the Japanese current and coming down from Alaska was so bitterly cold that in mid-summer a person's life expectancy still could be counted in minutes—a dozen or so. Riptides dragged logs and tourists out to sea every year. Up in the more heavily touristed sections like Newport and Lincoln City, they lost a half dozen tourists every summer.

Surfers flocked to these beaches, and the incautious ones were battered against reefs of volcanic rock even less forgiving than coral. Tides climbed ten feet up and down the beaches marooning the incautious beachcomber in rapidly narrowing coves surrounded by harsh cliffs.

To the north of the outlet of Eagle Cove, a great sea stack of dark basalt smeared white with bird guano rose from the thrashing waves. It was home to cormorants, common murres, and, most popularly, to over sixty pairs of puffins who came to Eagle Cove each summer for the breeding season. They favored deep rocky burrows high on the big sea stack just offshore from the outlet of the Eagle River. It was July and they'd be there now, each nursing their single egg. Soon the pufflings would break out and mayhem would reign up and down the length of the cliffs.

Jessica knew every nuance of this beach, even the fact that it never stopped changing from day to day. A strong wave came up the beach, but the tide was out and it didn't quite reach her.

Why had it taken a trip to Eagle Cove to realize that her Chicago career, if not in shambles, was not doing well. The days of merely being a good journalist was no longer enough. You needed a blog and a powerful, multi-threaded social media presence. She was paid to write for a living, but now she was supposed to give her writing away for free so that she'd accumulate enough of a following for someone to pay her. Totally backwards.

Besides, it wasn't working. The new car had gone on hold. The condo of her own was still stuck in a roommate budget—that was even after her dreams had diminished to a damn small condo. Takeout was Moon's Sandwich Shop or a slice of Chicago deep-dish rather than The Cotton Duck or a table at Antico. The flight to the wedding would be a budgetary strain that would take a month or more to backfill.

"It's all screwed up, Mom." Jessica hadn't even known that was true until she said it aloud.

"I know, dear."

She turned to her mother, "You know?"

"Of course. Just because I'm fifty-five doesn't mean that I wasn't ever thirty-two. At least I wasn't single— Oh, sorry about that, Jessica. But it's true, even though that's how old I was the first time I divorced your father. You were nine and I woke up one morning and couldn't understand how I'd ended up still in Eagle Cove and married to him."

"But Dad was always a good man, wasn't he?" Jessica dug her toes deeper into the cool sand that was rapidly making her feet cold despite the warm day. Of course a warm summer's day on the coast was barely seventy degrees; Chicago had hit ninety-three by the time she'd gotten on the plane early this morning.

"He's the very best, which is why I married him." Then her mother offered one of her wry smiles. "That's why I married him every time."

Jessica looked back out to sea. She'd never met a man who was "very best" and after playing the field in a dozen different cities across America and a few in Canada, she'd become convinced that such a man didn't exist out there.

And as if she'd needed Greg Slater to remind her, such a man certainly didn't exist in Eagle Cove.

# # #

Greg set out the ingredients for a simple roulade sponge base of flour, milk, butter, and eggs. He separated and whisked the yolks and set the whites to beat in the mixer.

The Puffin Dinner was now closed and quiet for the day. He loved the peace of cooking, using only one light over the stove and another over the prep table. The dining room was shielded from the midday sun by the deep porch and let him imagine its shadowed interior just waiting for the eager crowd to come.

Once he had the roux built, he folded in the egg whites, but the oven wasn't up to temperature yet. He could afford to wait a few minutes.

For the filling he mixed together some Italian Parmesan cheese and a couple cups of the goat yogurt that Tiffany made on her farm up in the woods. Her boyfriend had dragged her to Eagle Cove a couple of years back. They'd bought a chunk of property back above Orca Head that no one in their right mind would want, including her boyfriend. He left her there in the teepee they'd erected together and driven off to parts unknown. Tiffany had stuck. She'd cleared land, planted a garden, and bought a pregnant goat and a pregnant sheep.

It always surprised him each time she showed up in town. She'd come walking in—because it was her truck the boyfriend had driven on his way out of town—wearing worn corduroys, a flannel shirt, and a big straw hat atop her waist-length soft brown hair. She'd also wear a backpack sometimes with little bottles of goat milk, sometimes with containers of huckleberries or perfect heads of lettuce.

Tiffany mostly talked to herself, but they were lively conversations. And at times when Greg had been buying some of her products which were always fresh and well made, he overheard enough to learn that she was quite funny, often laughing at her own jokes.

The one time he'd joined in on her laugh at a particularly funny observation about seagulls' mentoring habits for their young, she'd stopped and studied him with dark eyes from beneath the wide hat. Then, she'd pocketed the money, not nodding her thanks this time (which was a fifty-fifty proposition at best), and wandered down the street to the hardware or grocery store before walking the two miles to the end of LBB Lane and then a mile or more back up into the forested hills behind Orca Head Lighthouse.

Greg dug parsley and scallions out of the walk-in fridge and began to chiffonade them on the maple chopping block. The only sounds were the quick snicking sound of his knife and the occasional ping from the oven's warming metal.

There was a lot of speculation among the townsfolk about what they'd find if they went up to Tiffany's farm. The few adventurous souls who had tried quickly learned that she was a crack shot with a bow and arrow which discouraged any active interest, if not the idle speculation.

Nicky Vance had bought himself one of those high-end camera drones for himself last Christmas.

"I'll do flyovers for Mrs. Baxter's real estate listings, and adventure videos for the whale tours and fishing trips. This sucker will pay for itself in weeks," he'd patted it proudly on the head.

On his first town flyover, he flew a circle around the Orca Head lighthouse. Then he decided to see just what *was* going on up on the cleared patch in the forest beyond. They'd all been huddled around him when he flew toward Tiffany's place. There had only been two really clear images. The first was a wide open clearing with animal pens, though no sign of a teepee or other house. There had been no time to zoom in before the second clear image was captured and transmitted back to them from the small onboard camera. The last frame of video the drone ever captured was the head of an arrow the moment before it hit. That night, the remains of the three thousand dollar machine had been staked to Nicky's front door with a second arrow through its heart—and most of the way through the thick wood.

Tiffany's ability with a bow also explained the time she'd brought Greg a thirty-pound slab of fresh bear meat. When he'd later asked if she had any more bear meat she could bring down on the next trip, she'd answered "Too salty for you" and gone on her way. Six months later, after he'd forgotten the whole incident, she'd given him a single pound of bear jerky. He'd shared it with the Judge who decreed, "Girl has finally got it right." It was the only bear jerky Greg had ever had, but it had been damn good.

He'd had a fantasy or two about Tiffany. She was pretty, at least everything that wasn't hidden by that oversized sunhat and hippie-loose clothing, and she smelled of pine and fresh river water. Perhaps a little younger than his twenty-nine, perhaps a little older, it was hard to tell. But as she spoke no more to him than to anybody else in town, he didn't see any point in trying to see if that fantasy led anywhere. But she was almost as intriguing an enigma as Jessica Baxt—

After a few trial sniffs, Greg sprinkled a little coriander into the yogurt and greens mixture and then poured it into the still uncooked sponge mixture.

"Crap!" His voice echoed about the silent kitchen.

He'd utterly ruined both.

Well, the oven now had plenty of time to reach temperature.

He scraped everything into the trash and started over on his second sponge base of the morning. He had plenty of eggs, but he was running low on yogurt and Tiffany's was exceptional. It had a tang without being goaty that would make a fine match for the flavor profile he was after. He made a mental note to buy extra yogurt the next time she came down the mountain. And maybe this time he'd try chatting Jessica up.

Jessica?

He scorched the flour and butter roux that lay at the heart of the roulade past golden brown and well into molasses-brown.

How had Jessica gotten in there?

He poured in milk to try and rescue the roux and ended up scalding the milk. By the time he had dumped that out and scrubbed off the brown layer glued to the bottom of the pot, the air had come back out of the egg whites and the whole thing had to be scrapped again. He'd made hundreds of roulade sponges over the years; this was Chef 101.

All he'd been doing was having a happy little never-going-to-happen fantasy about the local mystery girl and Jessica Baxter had floated into the diner's kitchen uninvited.

Greg glanced around, but there was just him and the second ruined roulade. With a sigh he started cleaning that one up as well.

Jessica had always been a knockout. He used to hide up on the dunes just to watch her run on the beach each afternoon along with the rest of the women's high school track-and-field team—half a head taller than any others except her cousin and running as if born to it.

Out of goat yogurt, he substituted cottage cheese in the third roulade which completely ruined the balance of Parmesan and coriander. When he caught himself reaching for cumin, he knew he was losing his mind. With slow and methodical care, Greg scraped the third mess into the garbage. The smoked salmon that Ralph Baxter had sold him wouldn't spoil. The scallops, still sitting in a bag in his seawater tank to keep them fresh, would live another day.

He needed air before he suffocated.

Out the back of the diner, he just started walking. It was early afternoon and his stomach growled to remind him that he'd missed lunch. He was almost to his destination before he figured out where he was going.

Greg was less than a hundred yards from Vincent's place when he heard the shout.

"Your head is up your ass, Vin. Go on! Keep it there!"

Greg hesitated for a moment and then kept walking forward, figuring he'd better go and see what was up.

Vincent McCall was standing like a cornered bull—or maybe a cornered bulldog…a puppy—in front of the rolled up door to his two-car garage turned woodworking shop. The space was so crammed with projects and lumber that Vincent had to pull his table and chop saws out under the eaves every time he wanted to make a new piece of furniture.

What had cornered him was Dawn McCall. She'd been hot since fifth grade when her body had decided she was done with being a kid.

Now at twenty-nine the view of her back had gone from attention-grabbing to awesome. Two kids showed nowhere on her hips. It was the ultimate joke that the school's soccer captain had become the stay-at-home dad and the girl that most had thought was the tramp of the school had become the most beloved science teacher at Puffin High. Of course it didn't take much imagination to understand why the boys all loved her.

Vincent glanced in Greg's direction in vain hope. No way was Greg dumb enough to take on Daw—

"And don't think I don't know you're back there thinking thoughts, Gregory Slater!" Dawn didn't even bother to turn to glare at him.

Shit! He hadn't meant to be thinking thoughts about his best friend's wife; it was just hard not to. She was the antithesis to Jessica Baxter. Dawn's curves just reached out and grabbed a man by his balls. He'd bet that her thick brunette ponytail, sparkling blue eyes, and killer figure dumbfounded every teenage boy trying to focus on the equations behind electron orbitals or celestial spectra, or any of the rest of that stuff that she'd distracted *him* from when they shared those classes over a decade ago. Her looks were a hard slap whereas Jessica's were a soft caress.

The funny thing was that Dawn's personality was normally soft and gentle whereas Jessica's was clearly pure osprey—one of the biggest predators of the coastal bird community.

Not holding true at the moment. Vincent was looking at him wide-eyed and desperate. Dawn didn't have much of a temper, but when it did cook off, it could be lethal. She was way smarter than either of them separately, but sometimes when they joined forces they could get around her. Vincent had pulled his butt out of scrapes often enough, so Greg took the risk and stepped forward.

"Sorry, Dawn. Sometimes I just forget what a lucky bastard Vincent is that he married you."

"Remind *him* of that," she pointed an accusing finger at her husband. "I'm going to pick up the girls at Mom's and we're out of here." The twin girls were the perfect second-grade spitting image of their mother, who had been vivacious even before her body had developed. The town's seven-year old boys were already in twice as much trouble as he and Vincent had gone through with Dawn. *Good luck, little guys.*

Dawn stalked over to her SUV and roared off in a flurry of dirt and gravel, which was particularly messy after last night's rain storm. Greg ducked too late and was spattered with mud right along with Vincent. Her tires jumped from driveway to paved lane with a jerk and a sharp squeak of rubber that left a dark black stripe on the wet pavement and had old Mrs. Winslow checking out her window to stare at the two of them for a long moment.

There was the other side of second grade; Dragon Winslow had been the terror of every seven-year old in town since before the dinosaurs had walked the earth.

Greg decided that he'd harassed Dawn and Vincent recently enough about living across the street from their old terror of a second-grade teacher to let it go this time. Besides, standing here beneath the Dragon's evil eye, it felt as if she'd somehow know if he did.

Greg brushed at his clothes. Between Jessica and her syrup and ketchup plate down his pants and Dawn's muddy departure, he'd definitely have to do a load of laundry sooner rather than later.

"What the hell, buddy?"

"Sorry, Greg. The woman works like a demon for nine months of the year and then once school lets out she expects me to take time off during *my* busy season to go to a movie and shopping up in Newport. No notice on a family outing…that she insists the girls told me all about last night. The two girls talk so fast when they get going in unison that I don't catch half of what they're saying no matter how I try. Dawn also wasn't too pleased about the Kriegson's place."

"The Kriegson's—" Greg had to do a real brain shift to navigate that turn in the conversation. "You got the contract?"

Vincent nodded sadly.

"But that's huge! Shouldn't be surprised, because you're the best custom furniture guy around. You figured it would go to that those guys out of Portland. So why the sad-dog face, Dawg?"

"The timeline. These summerfolk want everything by yesterday. It's enough money to carry me right through the winter and shove a chunk into the twin's college fund, but…" he waved a hand at the stacks of lumber in the garage.

Greg finally focused on what was crowding the shop. It wasn't local pine with a bit of oak trim. It was oak, maple, and cherry.

"The trim is all exotics and won't be here for another week. It's going to take the guts out of my summer with the girls and even worse, delivery is right when my folks are visiting and you know the Kriegsons are going to want a thousand little changes that they claim will only take a minute."

"Okay," Greg knew enough about Dawn and her mother-in-law to feel Vincent's pain; without Vincent available to act as a buffer between the two women it was going to be ugly. "I'm already dirty. Let me give you a hand."

"Oh, dude!" Vincent held up a fist in thanks.

"Dude!" Greg replied with a fist-to-fist punch hard enough that they were both shaking their hands in pain. It wouldn't be his pal Vin if it didn't hurt.

They picked up the first big board, Greg's hand still zinging a little, but it made up for not teasing Vincent about Mrs. Winslow.

Vincent maneuvered his end over toward the sawhorses. "You know, I saw Jessica Baxter driving into town with her mom this morning."

Greg dropped the board and barely managed to rescue his toe before it hit.

The end of the board bounced off a concrete block and the end of it split.

"Oh dude," Vincent said sadly, clearly not referring to the dropped board. He was the only person Greg had ever told about his teenage crush. Though of course everything Vincent knew, Dawn knew as well. "You're so goddamn pitiful."

"Tell me about it."

And like a true friend, Vincent ignored the wry tone and began to do exactly that, fully relishing every dumb detail Greg had ever admitted to.

Shit!

# # #

Jessica could have spent the entire day simply standing with her feet planted in the sand of the main beach, except she'd forgotten how cold the coast could be on a summer day.

Freshwater runoff from last night's rain was slipping to sea just below the surface of the sand, rapidly turning her feet into ice cubes. A thin fog was sneaking over the water and toward the beach. The inland Willamette Valley on the other side of the Coast Range must be heating up to drag the fog in off the water even at midday. And then the first wave of the rising tide reached her ankles and she yelped. The Pacific Ocean was damned cold.

She scooted up the beach to get clear of the next wave. Her mother was wisely back at the car, well clear of the rising tide. She'd also pulled on a light jacket the color of their eyes. Jessica might have to steal that one. It was irritating, useful but irritating, that her mom had better taste in clothes than she did. And she'd have to steal it soon, the fog wasn't put off by her Second City Improv Annual Revue t-shirt.

Even fifty feet from the beach the air was warmer, but not enough. As they got in the car, her mother spoke the old mandate, "Sand stays…"

"…outside the car. I haven't forgotten." Jessica did her best to dust off her feet but they were wet and sandy to the ankles and most of what she brushed off stuck to her hands. Soon it was like one of those oozing metallic encapsulations in science fiction movies, where the heroine barely has time to scream before becoming completely covered.

Her mother sighed when Jessica gave it up as a bad cause and pulled her feet aboard.

"Just like always, we're going to have to hose you down when we get to Gina's."

Jessica no longer felt twelve. The shift had occurred when… she was sparring with Greg Slater. Handsome men did have their uses, even when they were from Eagle Cove.

Her mother drove them up the winding lane toward the last house in town. A pair of massive Victorians dominated the south end of the beach before it was completely bookended by the rocky prominence of Orca Head. There was the Judge's place and then Aunt Gina's massive Lamont B&B.

"What's his story, anyway?"

"Whose, dear?"

When an eye roll didn't elicit any better response because of her mother's depressing habit of looking where she was driving, Jessica finally spoke his name.

"What about Greg?"

"Now you're being obtuse on purpose, Mom."

"Me?" She offered in a sweet tone that was so innocent that Jessica almost believed it. It was a tone from her childhood that Jessica had never been able to cultivate despite a fair amount of practice.

"Mo-om!" She said in her complaining teenage voice and they both had a laugh over it. "Did Greg even make it out of high school? Can't he do anything more than wait tables for his dad? How lame is that."

"Greg is—" Her cell phone rang. Her mother slipped it into the no-hands rig even though they were on a country lane moving about ten miles an hour.

"Hi, honey," Dad's voice boomed enthusiastically out of the speaker. "Is our little girl here yet?"

"Hi, Daddy," Jessica called out.

"Hey, Squirt!"

If she'd been twelve before, now she was feeling five and waiting at the dock for her father's boat to come back in.

"We're just on our way to Gina's now." Classic Mom didn't accelerate on the straightaway past the Slater spread.

Jessica stared at it as they slid by. The main house was almost as much of a monster as her family's home. When she was a little girl Judge Slater had added a mother-in-law unit that mirrored the grand house in miniature: a complete match down to small turrets and impossibly steep conical roofs. It had always struck her as so cute and cozy, even though she'd only been in it a few times during Grandma Slater's last years.

"I caught a monster halibut," her father's big voice filled the car. "Sold half to a customer who got skunked. Just got close enough to shore for the cell to work and called Greg. Must say that he sounded pretty damned relieved when I reached him. Any idea what that's about?"

"No idea at all," but her mother eyed Jessica as if she was somehow the cause.

"He took the other half," her dad announced.

"Wonderful. I'll get word out."

"Can't wait to be married to you again, honeybunch."

"Last time, I promise, Ralph."

"I'll hold you to that," her father's oversized personality shifted to a soft caress over the airwaves, making it a private joke. One so intimate that Jessica could feel herself blushing for overhearing.

"Still a couple hours to dock," his normal boom was back. "I promised the tourists I'd swing them by the puffin nesting grounds out at Chickadee Rock."

May through August they were thick with a hundred or more foot-high birds with brilliant orange beaks. Right now the pufflings were fledging and the parents were scrambling about the sky and diving hundreds of feet into the ocean to keep them fed. It really was a grand sight.

"I'll come and fetch you both as soon as I'm ashore and cleaned up. Bye, my honeys," and he was gone.

"What does Greg Slater have to do with Dad catching a halibut?"

"He—" Then her mother actually looked away from the road even though the last curve was close ahead. She looked straight at Jessica for a long moment.

"What?"

Then her mother offered one of her radiant smiles. "You want to know what Greg does? Fine. Keep your questions until tonight and they'll all be answered."

"I don't want to know that badly."

"Oh, Jessica. Of course you do."

# # #

Greg's level of distraction was high enough that he wasn't sure who was more relieved by Ralph Baxter's call about the halibut, him or Vincent. He hadn't dropped or damaged any more boards, but he'd knocked himself to the ground twice by catching his foot on the sawhorses. And he'd spent twenty minutes trying to round up the box of screws he'd knocked onto the garage floor. They were stainless steel, so he couldn't even use a magnet to gather them back up out of the sawdust. The sharp points pricked like blackberry thorns as he scrabbled about in search of them.

And every stupid-ass thing Greg did, his best friend had just rubbed it in more.

"Give me a break, Vincent. I don't even know who Jessica Baxter is anymore."

"Oh, like you knew so much then. But you've been pining after her pretty ass for every one of the fourteen years she's been gone."

"No, I haven't!" *Yes, I have.* "How do you know it's pretty? You said you just saw her drive by."

"Because it was awesome in a slim girl way when she was eighteen and you're *way* distracted now, dude." *Dude* had gone out of fashion when they were in middle school, so it had become their trademark greeting. Their theory had been that they were both out of the mainstream anyway, so maybe they'd become cool for being so *far* out of it. It hadn't really worked out that way. Though some part of it must have worked for Vincent, he'd married Dawn after all. By the end of high school, she wasn't just the hot chick, she was the hottest "get" as well. Beauty and brains joined together in a female Puffling. And despite all of the rumors, she'd been picky as hell—even if she had been dumb enough to pick Greg's best friend.

There'd never been heat between he and Dawn. Plenty of admiration, he had been a teenage boy after all and Dawn had been, well, daunting. But the connection had always been as friends. Vincent had fallen under her spell early and never recovered, though he had been damned slow on the uptake. He didn't figure it out until Dawn had asked him to the Senior Prom, then he'd never looked back.

Greg had taken Vicki Highland, who had the romantic soul of a razor clam. After the prom, when everyone had been headed to a beach bonfire in tuxes and gowns, she'd asked for a ride home. "I've seen a bonfire beneath the stars before," she'd kissed his cheek and gone inside leaving him dumbfounded on the porch. She'd married an accountant in Salem and worked as his assistant and business manager. About right.

By the time Ralph Baxter's call came in, he and Vincent both decided that it was a saving grace that there was now a massive piece of fish coming into dock.

Greg called around. Dawn and the twins often helped him when he did one of his "Irregular Friday Dinners at The Puffin." Even at seven years old, the girls already could do a fine job of setting tables or making sure a pot was well watched; he could trust them with most of the stirring on a risotto now, though they'd have to trade off a couple times because it was a long process. But they were out of town. He sent Dawn a text to be sure to be back in time to eat and got back a thumb's up emoticon.

Gina would be busy with her niece. Could Jessica cook? Or was she now one of those urbanites who could "order takeout with the best of them?" He'd wager on the latter. He briefly considered Tiffany, but he had no way to reach her so it didn't matter anyway.

He called Peggy out at the small Eagle's Airfield that served a few locals and the occasional tourist with their own plane. She was rebuilding an old Stearman Model 4 biplane with the idea of offering fixed-wing flights to tourists in addition to her father's aged Bell 206 helicopter. Peggy was also a fair hand in the kitchen. Unable to reach any of his other "regulars" he finally called his dad.

"Hi, Dad. You've never helped me with my food before, but Ralph Baxter is bringing in a side of halibut for me and I can't find some of my regular folks. I was wondering if you could help out tonight? Actually starting pretty much right now. I know that it's short notice but I would really..." Greg got the impression that the Judge was just letting him ramble on until he was done. So Greg grabbed a clue off the shelf and shut up.

"All you had to do was ask, son."

"You'd have to do exactly what I tell you. This isn't an omelet or a stack of pancakes. This is—"

"Greg," the Judge cut him off this time. "Remember who taught you to cook."

"Ma did," and he felt the pain of her loss all over again. He'd learned a lot of technique since, but Ma had taught him all of the basics, especially the passion for food. She would have *loved* what he was doing which was sometimes the only thing that kept him going.

"Exactly. They didn't make me a judge for all of those years because I was stupid. You tell me what to do and I'll do my best to help."

Greg pulled the phone away to look at it, as if he could somehow see the mysterious man on the other end of the connection. It sounded like his father, it just didn't speak like him.

He reeled the phone back in.

"I'll see you there, Dad. And thanks."

"Uh-huh," neither positive nor negative, just an acknowledgement. Greg wondered if he should reprimand the Judge for "offering such a neutral sound of minimal form and a complete lack of content," but then the connection was cut off at the other end and he'd lost his opportunity to do so.

Greg was halfway down the driveway when he pulled up short and turned back to Vincent. "You bring Dawn and the girls to dinner. I'll make sure you get a table. And get her some goddamn flowers."

"Yes, sir, Mr. Chef, sir!" Vincent saluted him as if either of them had been in the Navy.

"And don't pick them from her own garden."

He could see by his somewhat abashed look, that's exactly what Vincent had been about to do. How Vincent had ended up married to Dawn was a mystery…to all three of them—well maybe not to Dawn, but he and Vincent had never figured it out. Then Vincent smiled that bad idea smile of his that had so frequently led their trio into disastrous trouble as teens.

"What?"

"I'll just slip over and pick them from Dragon Winslow's garden!"

Greg decided that scarcity was the better part of valor and made himself scarce very quickly. He just hoped that Vincent was still alive to bring his wife and the kids to The Puffin later tonight.

# # #

"Natya!" Jessica shrieked with delight. She jumped out of the car, not slowing down to close the door, and raced barefoot across the lawn. Jessica hadn't seen her cousin since she'd come through Chicago last year for a tech seminar.

"Jessica!" Natalya shrieked out their customary greeting in turn as she leapt down the front steps of the grand Lamont Victorian home.

They came together with a quick kiss and a hard hug that made Jessica feel like maybe it wasn't too weird to be home.

"I thought you were in Portland." Natalya was supposed to be there because then she'd be Jessica's secret refuge from the reality of Eagle Cove.

"I came down to help with the wedding."

"Didn't they tell you it had been delayed?"

"They did," and the way Natalya said it, Jessica knew that her friend had come down mostly to help Jessica survive the upcoming week.

"You're a true friend," Jessica whispered as she gave her another hard hug of thanks. They turned toward the house with their arms around each other's waists.

"Actually, the way I figure it, you're going to owe me big time. And don't think I won't collect." And she would. At four years old, Natalya always knew how to get someone in her debt and she never failed to make them pay. Of course, she was so damn pleasant about it that you wanted to anyway. Natalya had always been the slippery one who appeared to have the road ahead of her paved in gold, or at least a high-grade oil that eased her quickly on her way. She could lie with a straight face and no one ever seemed to care to prove her wrong.

Mom handed over Jessica's abandoned sandals then proceeded up the broad front stairs onto the verandah and headed inside.

Despite knowing better, Jessica had always fallen for every one of Natalya's traps and, worse, she'd never gotten away with anything. Just once in her life she'd like to really pull the wool over someone's eyes. She sighed. If it hadn't happened for her in the first thirty-two years, she wasn't going to bank on it in the next thirty-two.

She stopped at the bottom of the stairs and looked up at the grand old house.

It looked like…home.

The old Lamont homestead was a grand, glorious, and utterly charming place. In true Queen Anne style, it had a wrap-around verandah encircling most of the elevated first floor. The porch was safe from the heavy coastal rains beneath deep awnings which perched atop tall posts connected by ornate railings—safe except when the weather was driven sideways by the equally impressive coastal winds. Steep gables popped out of odd places with the least invitation and a great circular turret rose well clear of the second story to lord itself over the rest of the house. Small second-story balconies were tucked in odd corners. The roof and siding were black, the trim and porch rails were white, and the turret's pointy, dunce's cap roof was as bright orange as a puffin's beak in mating season—a color so bright that it didn't exist in the Crayola crayon box, not even the sixty-four set with the sharpener in the back.

Mom had moved into Dad's house thirty-five years ago and Aunt Gina had turned the home into a B&B, but much of Jessica's summers had been spent playing on the porch here—and later necking with boys here where Mom wasn't around to watch. Gina was more tolerant as long as Jessica or Natalya didn't go too far.

"So how's the grand voyager?" Natalya teased her.

"Glad to be home."

They both stumbled to a halt and looked at each other in surprise.

"Did I just say that?"

"You did," her mother swept back out of the house, deposited her knitting bag by a chair, and went back inside.

"No way did I say that."

Natalya was eyeing her closely, "Actually, Cousin, you did."

"Weird." They started up the porch steps together.

"Very weird."

"I think this calls for alcohol."

"Too early. But Mom had ice tea and lemonade made."

Glad to be home? Jessica felt depressed by the thought. Chicago was home.

It was almost as if for the next week the rules that so tightly bound her life had come unbound. Job? Who cared? It was a disaster anyway. Car? Safely at Chicago O'Hare airport in long-term parking. Cat? Belonged to her roommate.

"Stepping out of yourself from time to time isn't necessarily a bad thing."

Jessica twisted to see a woman she didn't know sitting in one of the porch's heavy Adirondack-style chairs. She had a round face with striking brown eyes that matched her gorgeous cascade of hair.

Just as Jessica's mother had made her wish to cut her hair, this woman made her want to grow it high-school long again.

She wore corduroys the color of summer leaves and a blouse of white cotton. A gigantic straw hat rested on the next chair over. She was knitting a vest on circular needles in an intricate Fair Isle pattern. The colors were tea-dyed brown background with accents of Kool-Aid dyed natural wool—the dusky purple of Grape Berry Splash and Dark Cherry if she remembered correctly.

Jessica may not have knit much since leaving Eagle Cove, but the Lamonts had always been a knitting family. Aunt Gina would never have tolerated kin going out in the world not knowing how to make at least socks and hats, though vests and sweaters were better. Jessica recognized both the color work and the skill of the nameless knitter: better than she was, about the same as Natalya, and not as skilled as Aunt Gina or her mom.

Jessica saw a second set of knitting dropped on another chair. Natalya was making an elegant cowl in lines of alternating dark gray and jewel tones with custom-dyed fingering yarn. Jessica hadn't even thought to bring her own knitting. She was halfway through a second mitten that she'd been feeling guilty about for at least six years.

"Hi, I'm Jessica."

"Tiffany." And she didn't offer anything else. In fact, she gave the impression of never having spoken in the first place, as if her bit of advice had simply manifested itself out of thin air.

"Have you been in town long?"

Tiffany held up two fingers, barely breaking her rhythm with the needles.

"Days, weeks, months, or geologic eras?"

That stopped her knitting and had her looking up. "No other options? Centuries? Milliseconds perhaps?"

Jessica shared a smile with Tiffany and then shook her own head in the negative.

"In that case I'll take 'since the world was young.'"

Natalya gathered up her own knitting and sat back down with all the style and grace that Jessica had never been able to muster, not even on a good day when she wasn't feeling both jetlagged and age-lagged. She showed no surprise at Tiffany's presence which meant it wasn't months that the woman had lived in town, because Jessica knew that Natalya hadn't been home in that time span. So Tiffany had been in Eagle Cove for two years.

Jessica sat between Tiffany and her mother's chair and began dusting one foot against the other. The gritty sand slowly shed off her skin.

"I put you in with Natalya," Aunt Gina came out on the porch bearing a big tray of glasses and cookies. "It is the high season after all—though I did keep it empty for tonight until your mother moved her wedding date at the last minute—but tomorrow we'll be full again and I knew you girls wouldn't mind." As soon as her hands were empty, she wrapped Jessica in a bone-crushing hug. Jessica returned it for all she was worth. Though her aunt looked to be the sort of woman who reeked of scotch, fast men, and faster cars, she smelled of her kitchen and Jessica had missed her horribly by not coming home these last several years.

Mom followed close behind with massive pitchers of ice tea and lemonade.

Jessica eyed the tray, "Even I can't eat that many cookies. Especially not right after one of the Judge's breakfasts." She rested a hand on her stomach for a moment in sympathy with it for how much good food she'd eaten, leaving nothing on her plate despite her typically sparse eating habits. Then she reached out, "But I will start with *one* chocolate chip."

"You'll have some help. It's Friday afternoon knitting, dear."

Another change. Before she could remark on it, a car crunched up the gravel driveway and three women climbed out. Melanie Andriessen who owned The Flicker and knew a little too much about Jessica's use of the back row of her theater during her senior year in high school, Andrea Martins in dirt-smeared jeans and a t-shirt advertising Eagle Cove's only landscaping business, and Mrs. Winslow.

Jessica couldn't help herself, she screamed again and raced back down the steps to hug her second-grade teacher. It had been her guidance that led Jessica into journalism. She looked little changed—perhaps her hair was gray rather than salt-and-pepper, but she'd never been one for "all that hiding your age nonsense."

And perhaps her face was a bit more lined—but she still stood every inch of her five-eight and looked as if she'd just come from a long hike, perhaps up Mount Rainier or maybe Everest. She had to be in her mid-sixties at least, but she still hadn't quite transitioned to the dubious honor of "she's a tough old bird."

Mrs. Winslow patted her on the back while they hugged, and was surreptitiously wiping at her eyes as she and Jessica climbed the stairs arm in arm. Jessica was feeling a little sniffly herself…and more than a little horrified. How in the world was she ever going to tell Mrs. Marjorie Winslow, a woman who had wrangled her way into being a front-line reporter in the last years of the Vietnam War, that her star pupil was on the brink of total failure? Jessica did her best to shove the question aside, but it wasn't shifting offstage nearly as easily as Jessica would like.

Soon they were all sitting together on the porch, and cookies and drink were headed around as knitting projects emerged. Her old classmate Becky Billings rolled up in her bright blue delivery van—"5B" it declared in gigantic letters, then underneath it read "Becky Billings BlueBird Brewery." They exchanged squeals and hugs as well. Becky had become "tight as bees" with Jessica and Natalya ever since the day they first met in preschool. It was like there was a small rip in the universe whenever the three of them were together and merry mayhem had always ensued. Others arrived, some of whom she knew, some not so much, until a dozen women were gathered on the B&B's spacious front porch.

Mom dug out a spare set of number six straight needles and a ball of Lamb's Pride worsted in a soft butterscotch gold and another of light woodland green.

"Why don't you make yourself a nice scarf for when you go back to Chicago, dear?" As if she couldn't manage anything more complex than a scarf. She was on the verge of taking umbrage when she looked down at the needles. Jessica had to squint at them a little to remember how to cast on. Maybe she'd keep her mouth shut for a change.

She put the first slip-knot loop over her needle and then caught a very slight headshake from Tiffany, more an unexpected ripple of hair than a headshake. Making it look casual, Tiffany took the tail of her own yarn and slid it out to arm's length.

Right.

As subtly as she could, Jessica undid the slip knot, pulled out an extra three feet of yarn and made another knot; the long tail would be absorbed during the cast on. She'd have discovered the problem herself in a dozen stitches, but she'd been saved the embarrassment of pulling it out and starting over properly. No one else seemed to notice except Natalya, who was grinning at her like a co-conspirator in an international crime. Jessica offered a nod of thanks that Tiffany returned infinitesimally before turning her attention back to her own project. Jessica stuck her tongue out at her cousin.

So, whoever Tiffany might be, she missed nothing. That had always been one of Jessica's strengths, too. Natalya was the slippery one of the team, Becky the rowdy, and Jessica the observant one. They'd often agreed that what they'd been lacking was a smart one. She'd have to wait and see about Tiffany.

Wait and see?

What in the world was she thinking?

This was Eagle Cove and she'd be gone just as fast as her mother's wedding allowed.

# # #

Greg waded into "the zone" on occasion as much by chance as by planning. Sometimes it was a smooth slide, other times a heart-stopping plunge as bad as when the surfboard dumped him into the ocean and the wave action didn't release him until his head ached with the cold.

Tonight there'd been too little warning for him to be anywhere else except the zone. By the time the seventy-pound slab of cleaned halibut, Airport Peggy, and the Judge all arrived at the restaurant, prep time had already been tight.

In minutes he was spewing out directions like a master chef. He was so wound up that he slid into his commercial kitchen mode. He only ground to a halt when Peggy came to stand directly in his path and wouldn't let him by to reach the fresh herbs he kept growing in the restaurant's south window.

"What?" He snapped at her.

Peggy stood still. She was half a foot shorter than he was… and could snap him over her knee if she'd felt like it. She should have been an Alaskan bush pilot. Not like Maggie O'Connell in *Northern Exposure,* delicate for all her bravado. Peggy Naron was shorter than the model who had played Maggie and not much bigger around. But Peggy gave the distinct impression that if she had to wrestle a polar bear, it was going to be a bad day for the bear. She had dark curly hair pulled back in one of those ponytails that exploded behind the rubber band making it look as if she was racing in his direction just the way a diving eagle might moments before it killed its puny prey. She was closer to the Judge's age than his own, finishing high school while he'd been starting diapers.

"What?" He managed to tone it down this time.

"I've known you since you were still inside your mama, Greg. Babysat when she needed a break from you and Harry. Now answer me one question straight and I'll let you by."

What was it with tricky women today? First Jessica, then Dawn, and now Peggy. "Okay," he said cautiously.

"Where are you right now, Greg?"

"The Puffin Diner." He tossed it out as a joke, then wondered if he was about to get another plate of greasy food down his pants for being so flippant. How else was he supposed to answer such a weird question?

"Good boy. Remember that," and, that simply, she stepped aside. She returned to her work of shelling the scallops with knife and spoon. At least he hadn't wasted the beautiful shellfish on some earlier test just for himself; they'd be perfect in tonight's dinner.

He'd been moving so fast that, having come to a halt, there was an inertia against moving again. He glanced at his father. The Judge had been shaving shallots on a mandoline, but now had stopped. He wasn't watching Greg, instead he was looking at Peggy. Inscrutable as ever, there was no way to tell what he was thinking, and Greg wasn't sure if he wanted to know.

Then the Judge looked up at Greg and offered his "my decision is final" nod in obvious agreement.

I'm in the Puffin Diner?

Which meant what?

Oh! Duh! He wasn't in a pressure cooker like the Westin or The Herb Farm before that or the…he was in Eagle Cove, Oregon. He'd never enjoyed those high pressure kitchens, so why had tried to bring that attitude here? The only place more laid back than a small town on the Oregon Coast had probably been left behind along with the 1960s.

Greg hadn't done that on Friday night before, entering the commercial kitchen frame of mind, at least he hoped he hadn't. No, if he had, Dawn wouldn't have the least compunction about reaming his ass and she wouldn't have been half as gentle as Peggy had just been.

And the time pressure wasn't *that* bad. He glanced at his watch. Okay it *was* that bad, but that didn't make his manners any more excusable. Peggy and his father were helping him out of kindness; they wouldn't be paid much more than food. The twenty dollars *prix fixe* often barely covered the ingredients he used and the beers that he paired with them.

Yes, Oregon now boasted the number two wine region in the country, gaining ground on Napa, but for some reason all that changed when you crossed the Coast Range. Out here beer ruled. The first microbreweries of the new era had been founded in Oregon. Now you couldn't drive a dozen miles down the coast—except in the long wilderness gaps—without finding another master brewer with their own set of techniques and flavors. He'd worked a lot with Becky's flavors from her 5B brews and already knew exactly which pairings he'd use tonight… except with the dessert. Blackbird Porter or Deep Bay Stout? The porter. Just a four-ounce glass with the dessert—No! He'd go with tiny servings of the Espresso stout. Crap! Except he had no dessert. He needed a dessert to complete the meals' overall flavor profile and if he couldn't think of—

Calm. Take a breath. Be calm.

Yeah, right.

He was being totally stressed, but he couldn't dump that on his crew. He was trying to arrange the most complex dinner ever of his Irregular Fridays and there were so many elements to coordinate. He wanted to blame it on his father's presence, but the Judge had taken instruction well and without comment.

Yet still Greg couldn't move from where he stood rooted in the middle of the kitchen.

It was so important that this meal was utterly perfect because…

The first question he'd asked Ralph Baxter even before how much halibut he'd be bringing ashore was whether or not his daughter would be here tonight.

Vincent, who'd been standing close by, had slapped his back hard enough that Greg had almost lost his phone into the sawdust.

Ralph promised that he was calling his wife next to make sure all three of them were there. That's when the panic had settled over him nastier than a bar rag at the end of a busy night.

Greg took one last deep breath…and didn't feel cleansed at all. He could hear the scraping of metal spoon on scallop shell and the light tick of his father once again sliding the shallots back and forth on the mandoline to make paper thin slices.

He could do this.

He could make it good.

And it was as he rushed toward his window box herb patch that he understood the second level to Peggy's question.

Where are you, Greg?

He was in The Puffin Diner, though he preferred to think of it as The Puffin when he was serving fine dining here. He was in a kitchen that he knew better than any other in his past. And he was here to serve a meal to his family and friends.

His real goal however—absolutely proving just how totally lame he'd truly become—was to impress the hell out of a beautiful woman he hadn't seen in fourteen years.

# # #

"Why is everyone being so damned mysterious about this?" Jessica whispered to Natalya as she climbed the steps to The Puffin Diner for the second time today.

"Because it's making you crazy."

That was certainly the truth. Mom had simply declared, "Greg is doing a Friday night," which was greeted with a swell of excitement from the knitters, "and Jessica doesn't know what that means." That had elicited a half dozen "You're in for such a treat, dear," comments.

And when she'd pushed, they'd all shut down. When she'd tried being subtle about it Mrs. Winslow had snorted out a laugh at her lame technique and Tiffany had merely rolled her eyes. It reached the point where she couldn't even mention it tangentially without getting shut down.

"Are you going?" she'd asked Tiffany.

Before the quiet woman could even look up, the other women were once again telling her not to pry. After everyone else had returned to their knitting, Tiffany had glanced up and offered another one of her minimal, hair-rippling headshakes. A mouthed *why* had only elicited a widening of her eyes and an uncertain shrug.

Afterward, while Jessica had been inside clearing plates and glasses, Tiffany slipped quietly away to who knew where. There one moment and then gone.

"Doesn't talk much, does she?" Jessica had asked Mrs. Winslow when they had a moment alone.

"Only when the girl has something to say."

Jessica glanced over to see if that was a remonstrance of some sort. It had been in the second grade that Mrs. Winslow had taught her the first key to good journalism: "Shut up and let them talk." It was a skill that she'd had a hard time learning as a seven-year old, but after a year in Marjorie Winslow's class—often sitting isolated in the front left desk scooted well away from the others—she'd learned it well. But Mrs. Winslow's comment didn't appear to be accusatory this time, so she didn't mind the gentle reminder of the axiom.

When asked how soon she'd be ready to go to dinner, she'd shrugged that she already was.

In response, Natalya had grabbed her arm and dragged Jessica up to the room they'd be sharing.

"What?"

"We're going out to a nice dinner. You need to put on some finer duds, girlfriend."

"I thought it was just Greg doing something."

Natalya had merely shoved her toward her suitcase.

"Since when did people in Eagle Cove play dress up?" She received no answer as she started sorting through possibilities.

Oregon evenings grew chilly early, so she'd selected a pair of white linen slacks with just a hint of a flare, sandals with knit Christmas socks because she wanted to be fancier than her battered running shoes, but didn't want to risk messing up the only nice shoes that she'd brought for the wedding. She swiped a black denim shirt from Natalya, but it was warmer than she thought so she'd ended up tying the shirt tails together high on her midriff. A little skin never hurt. A filmy scarf of spring green borrowed from Aunt Gina had completed the outfit.

"Put a flower in my hair and I'll be certifiable," she whispered to Natalya as they climbed the steps to the diner.

"No, then you'd be perfect and that wouldn't be fair to the rest of us."

They stepped through the door arm in arm, and Jessica had to glance back to make sure that she hadn't just slipped through some kind of space-warp, time-portal thingy. But she hadn't; Beach Way was still behind her and a steady trickle of townsfolk were flocking this way.

She looked back at the room. Rather than harsh fluorescents and sunlight slamming onto battered Formica tables, the space was now lit by rows of twinkle lights running around each fluorescent fixture and tiny spotlights on Ma Slater's paintings. The tables had been transformed with midnight blue tablecloths, buff-colored napkins, and the soft oranges of the sun settling into the inevitable bank of fog that was forming far offshore.

"Maybe I'm certifiable without the flower in my hair."

# # #

Greg had been transfixed by the vision entering his restaurant. He'd been trying to find something to say, when he overheard her comment. He turned, selected a small dark-red dahlia from the vase that Vincent had dropped off to be a surprise at their family table—good man, he'd bought a nice arrangement that wouldn't miss the one bloom Greg had just liberated—and he nipped off most of the long stem with the chef's knife he kept sheathed on his hip.

"If I may?" He approached Jessica. While she'd stared at him in astonishment, he'd slid the palm-sized flower into her hair where she'd gathered it in a sidetail to flutter on one shoulder.

"There." It brightened her appearance, making her look even more exotic and other-worldly than she already did.

"Uh thanks. So, that makes me completely certifiable?" Her smile made him feel far taller than his eye-to-eye height.

"Absolutely. Certifiably lovely."

She snorted a laugh at him.

All he could do was grin in response. Even next to Natalya she was the standout in the room.

"Where do you want us, Greg?" Ralph Baxter looked the sea captain role. He stood six-two, fisherman-shouldered, and his own blond hair lightening toward white. He hovered protectively close to the women with him. He turned as Gina Lamont and Jessica's mother entered as well.

"I don't have a six-person table," Greg was looking around for which two tables to pull together, but there were only so many tables in The Puffin and he hated to turn anyone away. Next time he'd push them together in long, communal rows so that there wasn't a wasted seat.

"Oh, don't worry, dear," Gina hooked her arms around her daughter and her niece. "We'll just squeeze in all friendly-like at a four-person. Monica, you can just sit in Ralph's lap, you lovebirds."

Jessica rolled her eyes and Greg tried to smile at her in sympathy. But Gina's comment only reminded him of the unbearably sad scenes he'd witnessed as the Judge had tried to figure out how to say goodbye to his wife of thirty years—sometimes cradling her for hours in his lap though he clearly had few words to offer. Greg did his best to ignore that memory as well as Jessica's "And what the hell is your problem?" look by turning to seat the other arrivals.

Soon, The Puffin was crowded to the limit. In addition to the six stools at the counter, he had two couples standing at either end. He found a few more stools from the back and seated them behind the counter, facing their partners across too small a space. Next time he'd have to take reservations, perhaps even do two seatings. That was a first, which was absolutely incredible…and was freaking him out more than just a little. So many people, so many servings to do.

He took one last look about the room as he stood up from asking Vincent's twins about their outing to Newport. It had included a visit to the aquarium which was always a big hit:

Emma was more of a shark gal, Irma preferred the otter tank. Dawn looked only moderately harried from trying to satisfy them both. Vincent was doing a good job of getting the girls to tell him every detail and giving his wife a chance to breathe.

"How about next time, I go with you?" Greg told the twins. "Then when no one is looking, your dad and I can toss you both in to swim in the otter tank."

Beneath their squeals of fearful delight, Dawn whispered to him, "Thanks for the flowers."

"They're from—" he didn't get to finish.

"I've been married to Vincent for ten years and two children; I know who to thank, Greg."

"He means well," Greg did his best to reassure her. He'd never heard her as rough as she'd been this afternoon.

"Always," she said it with a sigh, but he could also hear that she really meant it which made him feel more relaxed about what was going on with his two closest friends.

Greg stepped away before Vincent could know that their flower-ploy was blown.

He headed for the service counter, bewildered by the miracle of everything that was happening. The restaurant was packed solid with people and they'd dressed up to come—as if this was important. There was a buzz of merry anticipation in the air. Fine dining in Eagle Cove.

It was enough to make him laugh, or hide in the back of the walk-in freezer and shudder with terror until they all went away.

Peggy began setting up the trays of Halibut-Scallop Ceviche appetizer and he served them out. He'd decided to use the heavy-bottomed wide Old Fashioned glasses he'd picked up cheap at a bar supply store. The thin slivers of red onion, the teasing microgreens, and the spheres of the dwarf cherry tomatoes made a nice contrast to the white halibut and pale scallops through the glass. He'd done all of the knife work on the fish himself, because first impressions were so important.

Becky came along behind him doing her brewmaster spiel and talking about the salmonberry pale ale as she poured just a few ounces into small juice glasses. She also had a soft cider that she served to Vincent's twins and those who wished it.

Greg didn't serve Jessica's table first, but he didn't serve it last either. A customer who received their meal mid-service didn't feel the guilt of being served first along with the boredom of waiting while others finished.

He was delivering one of the final trays close by Jessica's table when he heard her speak up, "When did the Judge get so fancy?"

He almost bobbled the last glass of ceviche into Dawn's lap. He managed to recover and offer her a smile.

So much for trying to impress Jessica. It felt as if his longest chef's knife had just been pounded in right between his shoulder blades. He abruptly wished she'd just go back where she came from. Why did she have to come back tonight of all nights? Gods, he sounded like a whiny Jewish Passover ceremony. *Why on this night of all nights do we…let our hearts think there's even a sliver of a chance?*

He turned for the kitchen to oversee the First Course and all he could hear was the roaring in his ears.

# # #

"Jessica, you idiot!"

"What?"

Natalya looked pissed. A glance around the table showed her parents and aunt were suddenly very focused on their glasses of ceviche. It was fantastic and by far the best food she'd ever had from the Judge. There was a lightness to all of the elements so that it didn't overwhelm the mild seafood, but rather complemented the bursts of tomato or the light zing of onion. It was bright without the usual ceviche problem of being too acidic.

"This is Greg's food, and he was standing right behind you when you said that."

Jessica hunched her shoulders as if he still was, even though she could see him back at the window.

"Greg can cook?"

"Oh my god," Natalya rolled her eyes. "Please tell me I'm not related to you."

"Since when can Greg cook?" She glanced surreptitiously to see him, but he didn't look any different. He was picking up a tray and Jessica could see the Judge right there in the kitchen. "But the Judge is the one cooking. Greg is just waiting tables."

"Odd," her father was rubbing his chin as if checking to see whether or not he'd shaved well enough. "I seem to recall selling that big halibut to Greg Baxter, not John. I'm not losing my mind, am I?" He aimed the last at his presently ex-wife, or maybe now she was his fiancé. That was her dad, always stepping in with a bit of humor to save the day. If Mom ever tried divorcing him again, Jessica was going to stage an intervention. As a matter of fact she'd make sure that the Judge had her phone number so she could tromp on it hard if it ever came up again.

"No more than normal, dear man," she patted his cheek affectionately. "We simply didn't tell Jessica about the treat she was in for."

"This is really Greg's cooking?" Some idiot part of her brain was having a particularly hard time with the concept. Cooking took skill and patience to learn which she couldn't reconcile with how firmly she had Greg Slater pegged as another Eagle Cove failure. She could feel Mrs. Winslow berating her for "preconceived notions have no place in a journalistic view."

The ceviche was more than good. It was a fine-dining chef's work; she'd interviewed any number of them over the years and knew that for certain.

She watched Greg move about the restaurant with a practiced ease. There had to be fifty people here and he didn't appear to hurry even once. It seemed that she watched him for a long time before she thought to ask the next question of her parents.

"Since when did Greg Baxter commit to anything?" That hadn't come out right. "I mean—"

"I," Greg was standing right by her elbow, causing her to practically leap out of her chair. He expertly balanced five plates of gorgeous fish, "spent two years at the CIA, apprenticed for two years at The French Laundry, and five years working with some of the finest chefs in Seattle. And how is *your* life going?"

He served them with only the barest of courtesy. Jessica half wondered if she was going to end up with a plate of fish down her blouse just as Greg had received hash browns down the pants from her. But he resisted whatever urge he was feeling, and stalked back to the kitchen. She noted with some chagrin that they were the last ones served this course.

Jessica looked down at her plate. It was just a simple piece of fish. Except it wasn't. The white halibut had a layer of herbs crisped on it. It flaked at the tiniest nudge with her fork and when she bit into it, her mouth was flooded with powerful flavors of chive, shallot, basil, and fresh parsley. The crisping of the herbs had added a bit of crunch and had muted the flavors just enough for the fish to shine through. The fish itself rested on a double swirl on the plate of strawberry and blueberry puree—as beautiful as art and so rich that every ingredient must have been fresh that morning.

A sip of Becky's Evergreen Lager—which thankfully didn't taste like pine trees—added a freshness that brought the fish completely to life. The roasted green beans were an attractive contrast.

"That's incredible. What the hell is he doing in Eagle Cove?" And Jessica could see she'd put her foot in it again. Why couldn't she stop doing that? She'd turned into an idiot with a dash of bitch thrown in and didn't like that side of herself at all.

"Okay," she tried again. "You all have lives here, I understand that. But the chef who can cook this could go anywhere. Anywhere." The next bite just melted on her tongue and she knew full well that she'd never have been able to afford the restaurant that someone like Greg would cook in, not even in her heyday as a rapidly rising journalist.

# # #

Greg overheard that as he was clearing the tables he'd served before hers.

He could go anywhere.

Somehow he knew that now. He hadn't until this moment, but he did now. Sure, these were Eagle Cove locals, but just because they were coastal didn't say what most people thought it did. A couple decades back, all of these little communities were busted flat logging or fishing towns—and some still were. But others, like Eagle Cove, were now tourist retreats and retirement communities. He was constantly astonished at what the people here had done before coming to live here.

And now he was the one astonishing Jessica Baxter and he liked the way that felt on several fronts.

As guests finished the crispy-herbed halibut, he replaced it with a coconut gelato palate cleanser served in tall martini glasses with tiny sugar-bowl spoons. The unexpected flavor, floated on just a dribble of Becky's hard cider, would jar their palates enough that they wouldn't be overwhelmed by three courses of seafood.

Watching their reactions, thanking them for the compliments, he knew that he *could* go and start his own restaurant, even make a go of it. If it wasn't for the money. He could solve the startup money issues with a partner, but he didn't want to be burdened by some other chef who would try messing with his recipes. And a manager-level partner would probably end up trying to manage the kitchen as well as the front of the house and that would never do. No, Greg wanted the control. He rather liked being his own master here at The Puffin.

He ducked into the kitchen to start working up the Second Course.

This was the trickiest of the lot and it took everything he, Peggy, and the Judge had to pull together the Halibut Veracruz. He left the floor to Becky's charm, which bubbled out of her as easily as the fizz in her cider, and focused on the food. The paper-thin slices of chorizo sausage had to be seared, but not burnt. The tomato-and-Spanish olive sauce had to be hot enough to finish cooking the intentionally underdone fish as it traveled to the table, yet the long curves of sliced avocado and the final dollop of sour cream must remain cool on the tongue.

"I knew you were good, son," the Judge spoke as he ladled the sauce over each piece of fish in the long line of plating that covered every available surface.

"He just had no idea how good," Peggy finished for him as she nestled in the thick slices of buttered and toasted French baguette from Cal's bakery.

Greg set the avocado and sour cream himself, checking that each plate looked perfect as he went.

"I'll give you whatever else you need," the Judge finished and began gathering up the first plates to carry out.

"What you're doing is just great, Dad."

"No, I mean whatever bankroll you need to get started, I'm your man," and he was gone from the kitchen his arms laden with plates.

For the second time tonight Greg's mind went into full lock-up—skidding sideways, unable to get his foot off the pedal. He knew he was headed for some kind of a crash, but he had no idea what it was or what he could do about it.

Peggy slapped his butt hard enough to jar him loose. "Damn, boy. You're almost as cute as your father when someone catches you out." And with a bark of laughter, she headed out with the next tray of food.

His own restaurant? It was finally in reach…and due to the most unlikely of sources.

# # #

Serrano chili, garlic, oregano, capers…it didn't matter that there was no salt and pepper on the table; the dish had been seasoned to perfection. The cherry porter harkened back to the sweet berry puree under the First Course without adding an unwanted sweetness to the Halibut Veracruz.

Jessica wanted to wallow in the dish: like a luxurious trip to the spa. It was an adventure of flavor and texture. She'd done some restaurant reviewing—had chiseled out a brief niche among the new chefs of Chicago, though the niche had gone away when some New York reviewer had decided to move to town to make their name, imitating the huge splash Cassidy Knowles had made in Seattle. But in those first six months she'd learned a lot about innovative food. Greg didn't innovate, at least not in the way most of them did. It wasn't all molecular techniques, odd foams, and food that had been manipulated until it looked like anything other than what it was.

He'd found his challenge in simplicity, a much harder technique. When the dish was simple, when it was designed to highlight just one or two key ingredients, then perfection was required. There was no hiding a flaw when the artist's palette was something as simple as a piece of mild white fish.

"For dessert," Greg announced to the room, "I made a chocolate-strawberry roulade with a hazelnut meringue. Becky has paired it with her Deep Bay Espresso Stout." Which Jessica was charmed to see served in little espresso cups.

"You can't ruin this one," Greg whispered to her as he served dessert to their table.

She looked up at him in surprise. Something had shifted in him during the course of the meal, and she didn't think it was just in her own perceptions. There had been a nervous energy about him; of worry, thinking back to it. This meal had scared him initially and she could see why, it had been a large and complex undertaking for such a small crew. But now he carried himself with a confidence, a surety that he had lacked before. It was as if the boy had become a man over the last hour or so.

"How would I have ruined it?"

Then Greg did something wholly unexpected, he blushed. Deeply, until she could see his face was bright red despite the subdued lighting from the twinkle lights.

"How…" Jessica trailed off unsure if she wanted the answer to that question.

"I had to toss three roulades in the trash this morning…" he too trailed off.

"Because of…" there was only one thing that Jessica could think of that would explain his reaction, "…of me?"

After trying twice to speak unsuccessfully, he nodded, offered a charming shrug of, "And there it is," then moved on to serve other tables.

Nobody at the table was studying their dessert this time, instead they were all looking at her.

Choosing discretion over stark embarrassment, she focused on her own dessert.

"Always knew he was sweet on someone—" her father's voice carried far too well. Thankfully Mom shushed him. Even in what he considered to be a whisper, Dad's voice still carried. "Well, it was as obvious as a hard bite on a long leader that there was some reason he never got serious with a girl."

"We just never knew who." At least Aunt Gina's whisper didn't carry past the table with how cozily crowded together they were, but it reached Jessica well enough.

"He's certainly never made a meal as good as this one before," her father's voice carried again and people at nearby tables started agreeing, and then a round of applause broke out.

Under cover of the applause, as Greg did a fine job of bowing and looking both humble and pleased, Natalya whispered to her. "And now we know exactly why he cooked like that as well." She offered a bawdy wink and a nudge with her knee where they'd been bumping each other under the small table all night.

Jessica could feel her ears going as hot as Greg's face had been. She reached up to release her hair from its sidetail so that she could hide a bit, but her fingers caught on the flower she'd forgotten all about—the one that Greg had tucked there.

Certifiably lovely.

Oh crap!

Once the buzz at the table turned to other topics, she looked up and spotted Greg. He was squatting down between Dawn—the freshman-year hussy—and the cutest pair of twins Jessica had ever seen. By how Dawn and the girls were dressed up, maybe that old hussy assessment had been wrong as well. Vincent McCall sat with them. She vaguely remembered Dawn, Vincent, and Greg being close in school; three years behind her, she actually hadn't given them much thought. Wouldn't have given Vincent any at all if Dad's best friend and fishing-and-crabbing buddy wasn't Danny McCall.

And back in the day Jessica had only noticed Greg separately from the others because he was Harry's little brother and had always been hanging around. As a matter of fact, he'd been a real pill to shed when she and Harry had been trying to finagle some alone time for experimenting. Greg had been a seriously tenacious little shit.

As if he knew that Jessica was thinking of him, he looked up from whatever the twins were telling him; looked right at her.

For the first time she didn't see Harry's little brother. Instead she saw a darkly handsome chef who had just served one of the finest meals of both their lives.

Chapter 3

Friday Night

T*he Judge didn't cook* on Saturdays or Sundays—*Don't much like damn tourists anyway*—so there was no urgent need to finish cleaning up The Puffin, but ten years of habit had Greg staying even after the others left. He liked making sure that everything was shipshape and tucked away.

He'd also enjoyed the chance to think about the night. He'd often received thanks and handshakes for his meals, but he'd never received a round of applause like that before.

He still didn't know what to make of his father's offer. His parents had set up a college fund that had seen him through the two years at CIA, plus the extra courses he'd crammed in during summers and weekends. The day he'd graduated the

Judge had taken him aside and handed him a check for ten thousand dollars.

"This is your startup fund, Greg. We gave the same to your brother. You work your ass off and you make this last. It's all there is until your mother and I pass. Not because we can't afford it, but because a man has to make his own way in the world and he won't do that if there's some damn safety net bailing him out every time he goes overboard." It was one of the longest speeches of the Judge's life.

Greg still had every cent of that original ten grand in a savings account. For ten years it had been the symbol of his own restaurant and he'd built on that, never once touching it. He hadn't done it fast. That money in the bank gave him a confidence that allowed him to work for less where he could learn more.

And his father had just broken his own rule and offered to bankroll his new restaurant. Greg had thought that was still two or three years away. He didn't want to squander the opportunity, so it was going to take some thinking and planning before he took any action at all. He'd treat it as a venture capitalist's investment which he would repay with very high interest.

One last check and he could find nothing else to clean or straighten. The kitchen stood ready for whatever came next—a blank template. He liked that. Unlike so many of the restaurants he'd worked, this one wasn't all pre-stocked for some repeat performance of a fixed menu. There wasn't a dinnertime's estimated stock of a dozen racks of lamb, fifteen lobster tails, twenty pounds of beef tenderloin ready to be made into filet mignon, and all of the other culinary traps of a successful restaurant.

His favorite part of any restaurant had always been the Fresh Sheet. What was at its very best *today*. What could be done with it. His Puffin's kitchen was like that. Nothing pre-decided. A halibut had been caught a dozen hours ago, reached his hands two hours later, and had now fed fifty-three people.

He patted the thousand dollars in his pocket. Even after paying back all of the vendors—because Ralph had comped him the fish in exchange for dinner for his family, making it a very expensive meal for Ralph—he'd have over seven hundred dollars which was going straight into his restaurant fund.

Lights out, he pulled the door shut behind him and turned to face the night. t was warm and the ocean freshness was thick on the air. The Flicker's marquee was out. The late show was done; it must be later than he thought. Usually it lit this entire end of Beach Way.

Everything was shadows.

Like most coastal towns, Eagle Cove had rolled up its sidewalks and only the Bobbin' Red Robin Tavern remained open, its neon sign advertising "5B Brews On Tap" as a muted statement in the front window that barely lit the stretch of sidewalk in front of it.

"What the hell, Slater?"

He jolted.

The voice, the tone, even the words themselves told him exactly who sat in one of the big wood chairs on the diner's dark porch. The three elements blended together made a nuanced statement even without the visual.

"Hi, Baxter," he wondered what Jessica was doing here. He'd bet that falling into his arms wasn't exactly likely.

His eyes had adapted enough to the dark to see her sitting in the second chair to the right of the diner's door. Greg could just make out the dark spot of the red dahlia that he'd tucked into her light hair. She still wore it. Had she been here since the patrons had left hours ago? Maybe, which was interesting.

He sat in the first chair and only in that moment could feel the familiar pounding of the blood in his feet. Restaurant work did that to you and it wouldn't be the end of a good day without that particular throb and ache. He kicked off his shoes, peeled his socks, and rested them on the cool, rough wood of the porch.

"Oh god, that feels so good."

"When did you start?"

"Today? After working for Dad from six to ten, I spent a couple hours helping Vincent with some cabinet work before your dad called with the halibut."

"Does he do that a lot? Or was it just because I was here?" He caught that the second part of the question was the important one, but answered the first.

"Some. I get fish from him. Danny McCall gets me crab when they're in. Tiffany brought me bear once, but more often sells me some elk."

"Tiffany? Quiet woman about my age with long hair? A good knitter?"

"She knits? I didn't know that. And she's definitely not quiet; she's always talking to herself—probably comes from living alone up in the woods. But the long hair fits. She's one of the best bow hunters in town. And you remember what they say about deer in this town…"

"Don't need a gun, just need a baseball bat." It came out in unison and they both laughed. He'd forgotten that Jessica Baxter had such an amazing laugh. The deer in Eagle Cove were so tame, that you could practically walk up and pet them.

"A lot of folk bring me venison whenever I need it. Beef in the fall from Mr. Greene… I get food from all sorts of folks in town."

"I actually meant how long have you been doing this?"

"Irregular Fridays at The Puffin or cooking?" *Or crazy about you?* But he wasn't going to say that one out loud. Or answer it.

"Both actually." In other words all three, but she wasn't any more willing to ask him about the unspoken part than he was to say it.

He wished he could see her more clearly than just her general location. She was facing him, in a casual posture that didn't place her hand on the chair arm next to his, but still she sat in an open way. In a…journalist's way. As a matter of fact, her questions were…

"Writing an article about me?"

"No. I just…" Jessica slipped into silence. When she spoke again, her tone had softened. "I don't know you, Greg. Everyone says that you're crazy about me, but you don't know me either."

"Making me just plain crazy." He slid down in his chair, extending out his feet until his toes were wiggling in the cool night air. "I can live with that."

Again that patented, secret sauce Jessica Baxter laugh.

He decided to go back to the first questions for safety. "Mom started teaching me to cook when I was tall enough to work on the counter while standing on a stool. I can't even remember when I didn't cook. What about you?"

# # #

"Cooking?" Jessica kept searching for some anchor in the conversation but wasn't having much luck. "I cook out of desperation, not skill. Mostly because my budget doesn't allow for a personal chef. Or even going out much for that matter." She hadn't mentioned that last bit to Natalya, never mind anyone else.

She'd been sitting here in the dark for hours trying to wrestle with that. Mrs. Wilson had seen clean through the thin facade that Jessica had been feeding her parents for a while now—along with everyone else who asked. Her mentor had been kind enough to not prod for details in front of the others, rather offering a kind "come and talk when you're ready" along with a hard hug.

Jessica had been feeding the story to herself as well. And the journalist who had been telling the story—herself—was good enough that she'd almost bought it.

It will turn around soon.

Just need a couple solid contracts.

Maybe get that big interview next week.

But she'd gotten the big interviews, as many as ever.

Jessica had landed the contracts too, more than many of her friends, but the terms had grown worse and worse with each one. The pay was going down and the draconian terms were worthy of the most heinous lawyer.

"My career is against the rails…" Worst, there were no signs of it turning around at all. "…and I don't see it turning around anytime soon. I also can't believe you're the one I'm telling this to. I haven't told this to anyone, only just figured it out while sitting here."

"I'm a little surprised myself."

"And yet I'm finding it comfortable to do so?" She hadn't meant it as a question.

"I'll take that as a good sign," his voice was lazily pleased as if of course he deserved whatever good came his way.

"Don't get cocky, Slater."

"Whatever you say, Baxter." Smug bastard.

"Never mind. Forget I said anything." She struggled out of the chair, stiff from not having moved in hours. She'd gotten cold despite the atypically warm evening. Her knees were a little wonky as she descended the steps.

"Hey! Wait a sec."

Jessica got her knees in order and turned right at the bottom of the steps because Greg was descending to her left. Wrong way. LBB Lane was at the other end of the main strip. But Greg was now between her and her escape. She kept going. She'd hit the beach and walk back that way. She could see ahead through the darkness, by how the docks floated, that the tide was down low. Good, there would be enough beach to walk on.

"Jessica?" Greg's voice came from so close that she jumped in surprise. The quarter moon that had been hidden by the deep eaves over The Puffin Diner's front porch offered enough light that she could see him clearly enough. He was barefoot and had moved very quietly.

She turned and continued toward the beach. The street was completely empty. There were a couple of cars parked down by the bar. Weekenders, because any local would have walked on such a beautiful night.

"Could you at least tell me what I said to send you running off so fast?" He was still following her. She decided that was a point in his favor, for not being scared off by the first flash of her temper—another thing she could thank Mom for. The way he'd asked it earned him another point.

"You didn't say anything wrong, you simply hit the nerve that I've been trying to ignore since the moment I crossed the goddamn Coast Range this morning." The high-water fish on the front of Grouse Hardware was way over her head as they walked Beach Way's faded yellow centerline. "Actually for a while before that too. Like you drove a spike into it."

"Ouch! I could break in here," he hooked a thumb toward the hardware store, "and grab a pair of pliers. Would that help?" He headed toward the dark and locked doors as if he really would.

She was in such a fume that for just a moment she thought he was being serious. "Okay!" She huffed out a breath. "Okay! I'm being foolish. If you're going to keep walking with me, please have the decency not to point that out again. I hate whining almost as much as I hate being ridiculous."

"Ridiculous?" Greg offered amiably and veered back across the lane to walk beside her toward the docks once more. "You want ridiculous, you should talk to my buddy Vincent. He doesn't even know to get his wife flowers when she's upset. Now that's ridiculous."

Greg, Dawn, and Vincent. And now the twins. "Does it bother you that she married Vincent rather than you?"

"Not really. Vincent was gone on her all the way back to kindergarten. I love her to death and would do anything for her, but there was never a click between us."

"Not what it looked like in high school."

"Hey, I do have a Y chromosome, you know. Dawn was a knock-out way early; still is. But she was always the level-headed one out of the three of us. Always knew what she wanted. Double major in physics and chemistry and she came back to marry a carpenter and teach the high school kids. How cool is that?

But it wasn't her I was crazy about." He stated the last as a blunt fact; again that supreme arrogance. No attempt to hide the fact or whisper it or keep his damn mouth shut.

Jessica closed her eyes; allowed herself the freedom of walking for a moment with her eyes closed. The gentle breeze off the ocean brushed across her eyelids and tugged lightly at her hair until it felt as if she was floating.

Floating for now, and about to drown.

She opened her eyes and there were the docks sticking out into the bay that was Eagle Cove. A half dozen fishing boats and three sailboats. Not a lot of sailors were willing to brave the reefs, sea stacks, and generally nasty weather of the Oregon Coast—a storm was just as likely to come crashing in tomorrow as a day of light winds and pleasant sun. And if she made one more goddamn metaphor about her suddenly storm-tossed life she was going to turn in her journalist's artistic license.

"Tell me something, Greg. Anything. Just get my mind out of the rut that it's in."

# # #

Greg considered the challenge. He'd never really imagined himself just walking along with Jessica Baxter. Of all the things he'd ever imagined with her, he'd never thought of something so simple.

He did wish he hadn't blurted out that she was the one he was crazy about, but it was truth and it was out there. He remembered Chef Manuel telling him, "Once you break the damned egg, let it go and move on." So, he'd said it. No taking it back.

The other thing he'd never expected from Jessica Baxter was the amount of distress she was showing. He'd always been attracted to her simple confidence. She'd walked down a high school hallway with an ease of passage, without tipping over into her being some kind of a queen bee. It was the same way she wrote. He had an online search alert that kicked him an e-mail of every article she published. Her written voice was as engaging as her spoken one—straight ahead, true, no evasion or softening of hard facts.

And here she was asking him to help her avoid whatever she was thinking. She looked so sad, rooted in place at the end of Beach Way and staring at the small working docks floating at the edge of Eagle Cove. Daring greatly, he rested a hand lightly on her lower back and turned her toward the beach. With just the slightest pressure he was able to get her moving again.

And from that brief contact, he could imagine how she would feel to hold. The warmth of her against palm and fingertips, the extra little pressure where her spine and the inside of his knuckles had lined up. The soft smoothness of the thin fabric of her blouse. The tip of his thumb had just brushed the lower edge of her bra's back strap.

Way too easy to imagine holding her close.

"There's a moment in cooking," he had no idea what he was going to say, but if he didn't speak soon, a sudden dryness might close this throat forever. "I'll wrestle with a dish a hundred times. I follow the recipe. I work the ingredients. I get to the point where if I eat another lobster-stuffed pork chop I'm sure that I'll die."

They moved down the concrete boat launch ramp until they reached the beach and then turned south. The town lay sleepily atop the bluff to their left. On the moonlit sand, giant driftwood logs looked ten times their size with their dark shadows. The sand was a mixture of tide-packed hard and wind-blown soft that tickled his feet.

And his shoes and socks were still on the diner's porch. Well, he wasn't leaving Jessica's side to go back and get them.

To their right, the ocean waves sparkled outward forever. The steady *whump* of waves hitting the sand then scraping up and down the beach kept them company. Seagulls slept on the sand as bright lumps, who scowled when "forced" to stand and step out of the humans' way. A few miles to the south, Orca Head lighthouse towered above the beach, casting its sweeping lights out across the water, but passing high above the beach and town—a guiding beacon that offered no illumination to their next steps.

The ocean breeze didn't draw on the infinite fresh air and sea salt to intrigue his nose. Instead, Jessica, walking just windward of him, scented the breeze like warm honey. Like…what in the hell had he been talking about?

Food. Tough guess. He was a chef after all. Pork chops. That was it.

"Then after a hundred meals of merely good," he continued, "and occasionally awful, something happens. I'll cook without looking at the recipe. After all, I've long since gleaned every scrap that the prior chef encoded in coarse-minced versus fine-diced and dash versus pinch. And maybe I'm in too much of a hurry to look at the recipe again. I just cook."

He tried to assess what Jessica was thinking, but she ambled along beside him watching the beach ahead. They were moving too slowly for it to be walking. They were like two old friends heading down the beach as somewhere to talk rather than actually heading anywhere.

"There's something that happens at that moment. I…" he tried to recapture what he'd felt while cooking tonight. "I was no longer just cooking. I was…"

Somehow they had stopped walking and were facing each other in the moonlight. The sliver of a moon was behind her and her face was cool skin and deep shadow, like a modernist painting of herself.

Well, if he was going to go down for anything, he might as well go down for the truth.

"I was cooking for you."

It wasn't something he could have said even this afternoon. But the Judge had been right; he'd never cooked like this before. After so many meals for himself, for the Judge, and for the town, he could now feel the difference. And some part of him knew now that he'd finally glimpsed how to be a chef rather than just a cook. He wouldn't be sliding backward anytime soon. Just as thoroughly as Jessica had ruined the morning's roulades, she'd *made* the dinner, but he owned that now.

Jessica watched him without blinking. No tilt of her head to show what she was thinking.

He waited, too tired to do anything else. Too certain that once again he'd utterly blown it.

"I'm going back to my original premise," her voice was as neutral as her expression.

Was it some journalist's tool? Never show your own emotions so that the interviewee must fill the void? Well, his voice was food, not words, and he'd spoken with everything there was inside him.

"My first question was, 'What the hell, Slater?' That still seems appropriate."

If she couldn't see it or couldn't let it in… Somehow he'd thought more of her. He'd given her all that he had and it hadn't been enough.

"You know what? You were right. Teenage crush, decade-long delusion, whatever. I hope you enjoyed the meal." And to hell with her and to hell with himself.

He turned to continue down the beach.

Jessica grabbed his sleeve.

He shook her off, surprising himself as much as her.

"Okay!" It came out as a shout that he couldn't seem to clamp down on. "I don't know who you are. You left this town fourteen years ago at a dead run and you think I'm a failure because I didn't. Well, I did leave. But after eight years I came back because my mother was dying and then my father needed me. And you know what happened? I discovered I liked it here."

Still that neutral damned expression.

He almost blasted her with the rest of it. That he knew it was still a stupid schoolboy crush, but it was one that even just the sight of her brought roaring back to life. He wasn't an idiot, except about Jessica Baxter. He—

Unable to face what he did and didn't know, he turned from her and headed down the beach. She didn't try to stop him this time.

He waded through one of the half-dozen little runoff streams that cut just inches deep across the sand. The chill water did nothing to slow his steps as he passed the small, sleepy hotels perched along the bluff. The cuffs of his jeans now slapped wetly at his ankles chafing the sand into his skin.

When he glanced back, Jessica was still standing there, a shimmering figure in the moonlight—as ephemeral as the waves and just as indifferent. Maybe he should go back and apologize or placate or something, but he didn't feel like it. He was only now putting together why he'd cooked the way he had. He hadn't even known it until he said it aloud and it scared the crap out of him. The food had always been his and his alone. No one should have the power to ruin roulades or create the best meal he'd ever put together.

And the worst fear—the one that had him practically sprinting down the beach—was that he was fooling himself and he'd never again be able to cook just for himself.

# # #

"Where have you been?" Natalya's sleepy mumble greeted Jessica as she tried to slip into the room without waking anyone.

"Hell," she whispered. "Just go back to sleep, Natya."

And for a blessed moment it appeared that's what she did. But after Jessica had washed her face, brushed her teeth, and found a nightshirt, she could see Natalya sitting up in her bed.

"Care to explain that one?"

"It's two a.m. my time," the hall clock had softly chimed midnight as she'd snuck in, again making her feel like a teen past curfew. "I had to catch an early flight. We can talk about it tomorrow."

"I thought you were maybe necking with Greg Slater."

"So not," Jessica shifted her bag and the rest of her clothes onto the floor and crawled into the other bed. Even though it was the high season, Aunt Gina had saved them one of the largest rooms which just fit a double and a single bed with a tiny nightstand between them. Natya, arriving first, had grabbed the double, of course, just as Jessica would have done.

"Then I'm guessing that you weren't having your way with his body either."

Jessica didn't bother to answer, just hugged her knees to her chest and was momentarily glad that she could see so little of the room. Aunt Gina had decorated by genre and she and Natalya were in the Sci-Fi room. The lone shaft of moonlight just now reaching in through the west facing windows lit a small side table with a foot-tall Princess Leia doll facing a pair of Lieutenant Uhuras: one classic and one reboot. The three miniature women and one life-size one watched her with shadowed gazes. Thankfully only the life-size one was expecting an answer.

"Tell me that isn't why you stayed behind after dinner."

"That isn't why I stayed behind after dinner."

"Shit!" Natalya didn't curse often, but she put some heat behind it when she did.

"Stop that. You'll shock Anne." Even though it was invisible in the darkness, Jessica knew that a poster of Anne Francis and Robby the Robot from *Forbidden Planet* hung above Natalya's bed. Linda Hamilton from *Terminator II* hung above Jessica's bed brandishing her massive machine gun and wrapped in crossed bandoliers of bullets implying a deep cleavage despite the military vest. Linda wouldn't give a rat's ass what Jessica said, so she was glad she'd ended up with this bed.

Natalya sighed, "Please tell me that you didn't yell at him."

"No. But he yelled at me."

"Did you deserve it?"

"I dunno," Jessica dragged the covers over her head. "Maybe," she told the darkness.

"Heard that!"

Crap! She could feel Linda glaring down at her as well.

Chapter 4

Saturday Morning

It was the weekend. Worse, it was damn early on a weekend morning. He should be sleeping in.

Yeah, that always worked well for him. Getting up five days a week at five to help his father at the diner didn't exactly train him to relax on a sunny summer morning. Greg knew that the Judge, a creature of habit, wouldn't stir from his bed before eight on a Saturday—the end of the BBC morning news.

Greg headed out for a run to clear his head. The beach was chilly despite the promise of a warm day. The fog had moved close ashore and though the sun had cleared the Coast Range, it wasn't high enough to clear the bluff and most of the beach still lay in cool shadow.

As was usual, he trotted south to the base of the cliffs atop which stood the Orca Head lighthouse. He did some stretches against the rock.

He glanced up at the Lamont place. That and his family's were the two great Victorians of the town, like side by side beacons; together they were as commanding of the shoreline as the lighthouse perched hundreds of feet above him.

He'd spent much of the night puzzling about why Jessica's question had ticked him off so much.

What the hell, Slater?

Seriously, what the hell? He'd practically drooled all over her. He'd insulted her for her wanting marshmallows in her hot chocolate and run hot and cold through both the dinner and the conversation afterward.

Hi, babe. Haven't seen you in fourteen years, but you're the love of my life. Wanta do it?

Okay, he hadn't been that bad…he hoped. But he sure hadn't been good.

Nine days—eight now—if he wanted to do something about it before she once again left Eagle Cove.

He leaned into his hamstring and felt the stretch tug all the way up to his exhausted brain.

After last night, wasn't much chance of that happening. *Let's impress her by yelling at her and calling her an idiot.* Actually, he was fairly sure that he'd been calling himself an idiot, but it probably hadn't come out that way.

He tried the other hamstring which was no better after tossing and turning through most of the night.

Well, it wasn't going to get any better than this.

He heard a faint call caught on the breeze.

Greg scanned the beach, but the nearest person out this early was Clarissa and Emilio Thompson a half mile down and tossing a ball for their dog.

The call was repeated, a little louder. It might have been his name.

He tracked it to the veranda on the Lamont place. A tall slender figure with blond hair was shouting his name and waving him over.

A thread of hope shivered through him, as chill and cutting as the fog that hung close offshore.

Run down the beach and ignore Jessica for eight days? Or go all in and see just what he could do to explain himself from last night in hopes of patching things up?

Well, since he'd already broken some eggs, he might as well see what he could make with them. Besides, no matter the danger, he didn't want to risk not seeing Jessica for another fourteen years. He had to try.

Acknowledging that he was probably being an idiot, Greg began trotting across the beach toward the stairs that led up the bluff to the Lamont's house.

# # #

Jessica jolted out of a dead sleep, the kind that only happened after her brain refused to shut off with the lights. Like a combination of drunk, hungover, and three-day old dishes. She'd laid awake for hours in a mashed-up collage of her stumbling career, the amazing meal, and Greg's harsh words—that she'd thoroughly earned. He seemed like a nice guy doing his best to be honest and she'd slapped him with "What the hell, Slater." Real nice. Jessica heard the grandfather clock downstairs chime two before she'd finally plummeting into true sleep.

She tried to shake off the dream that someone had been shouting Greg Slater's name. Someone with her own voice. Jessica really had to file a complaint with the dreams department for writing such a crappy story. Guy dreams were supposed to be about handsome and sexy ones who flowed with charm. Instead she'd woken from a dream of a handsome and sexy guy who scowled like a ticked-off golden retriever—all happy, then all sad, then all happy, then…

Scrubbing at her face did little to break the mental back loop; she did *not* want to be thinking about Greg Slater first thing in the morning.

A quick glance showed Natalya was already up and out. The window was open and the air was warm so Jessica dragged on some shorts, waved at Linda all armed to thrash some poor Terminator's ass, and headed downstairs in search of cocoa—with marshmallows, goddamn it, and to hell with Greg Slater.

Aunt Gina had an instant hot water tap, so Jessica went with powdered mix and stumbled out onto the porch clutching onto her mug for dear life.

Mom was standing at the porch rail looking down at…Greg Slater just climbing the last steps up from the beach.

Greg stopped and had that same damn smile that had earned him a plate of hash browns down his pants just yesterday. Short memory if he'd forgotten the dangers. He'd forgotten. His eyes tracked down her body.

"Sorry, but you can't blame me for smiling at this. You just can't, Jessica."

She looked down at herself. Her oversized nightshirt was dark blue with a faded pink declaration: *I'm a woman. What's your superpower?* And it was just long enough, barely, to completely hide the fact that she was wearing shorts—shorts that didn't hide all that much more than Greg's running togs did. He wore lime green Nikes, gym shorts that did reveal a very nicely muscled set of legs, and a t-shirt that said: *The rules of the kitchen: 1. The chef is always right. 2. See Rule #1. 3. See Rule #2.*

"Is that so?"

Greg looked down to see what t-shirt he'd dragged on and then grinned back up at her, "Ab-so-tively!"

"And…" she loved it when guys just set themselves up for failure, "…since we're not in a kitchen, does that mean that you're always wrong?"

"Jessica!" Mom said it more as a sigh than a reprimand. "I called Greg to come up to talk about the wedding."

"*You* called him?" She sipped her cocoa and the heat tried to kick start her brain. She'd started to wonder if he'd appeared in answer to her dream calling him, but it had been her mother. That was some comfort to her firm belief in how the world worked. Just as strongly as being in Eagle Cove chipped away at that world view.

Greg went up on his toes and leaned in close to peek into her mug. "Are there marshmallows in there?"

"Of course!" Then she glanced down, she'd forgotten them in her sleepy state. "Damn!"

Greg dropped back on his heels just too damn pleased with himself.

For being a woman she wasn't feeling very superpowerful this morning. She wasn't going to retreat, well not far. She settled onto the porch swing.

She considered doing the whole making-a-show thing of slowly crossing her legs and…being a complete bitch. Her mother had left a rumpled quilt on the swing and Jessica pulled it over her legs as she sat.

Greg settled at a small table by the rail.

Mom patted Jessica's knee through the cover.

Jessica sipped her cocoa and offered Greg her most pleasant smile as her mother offered coffee and went in to fetch it.

Now her question had changed to *What the Hell, Baxter?* She should be teasing him and making him suffer for thinking that a ludicrous high school crush could possibly still mean anything so many years later. But she *was* touched.

And she had even less idea *what the hell* about that, than her career.

# # #

Greg didn't know which was worse, having Jessica's long legs out in plain view, or having her wrapped up in the green-and-gold quilt, her sleep-tousled hair the color of the sun, and clutching her mug of cocoa like a life preserver. It was impossible that someone could look so good right after they woke up. It made it far too easy to imagine waking up next to her the morning after; then the one after that and…

Mrs. Baxter came back out of the door and dumped a handful of tiny marshmallows into Jessica's mug. She looked up at her mom with the radiant smile of a woman who loved her mom with all of her heart.

He knew—in that single flash of an instant he knew—that no matter what real-world facade of disaffected urbanite she wore, Jessica Baxter would do anything for her mother. She'd just revealed that the Jessica Baxter he'd fanaticized about all his life was real, not some illusion that he'd been fooling himself with. He might not know her, but he certainly knew what sort of person she was.

Greg forced himself back to the present as he thanked Mrs. Baxter for the cup of coffee, a nice contrast to the morning's coolness. Eight days. Yes, he could think of a lot of things to do over the next eight days. It was plenty of time. And if it wasn't enough, maybe his new restaurant would open in Chicago.

He looked away from Jessica, because he didn't want her to see what he was thinking about "their" future—not even a little. It was utterly insane, but he couldn't seem to stop himself, so like a good chef, he'd follow his instincts.

"We were going to keep it a simple affair," Mrs. Baxter sat shoulder to shoulder with her daughter, but declined to duck beneath the quilt making Jessica look even more cozy. "But May Conklin at The Brass Plover Pub is incredibly overbooked for any catering next weekend. Frankly she was overbooked for this weekend and was only going to do the wedding as a favor to me. So, I was wondering, Greg. Could you possibly cater the wedding next Saturday?"

"Sure," he agreed appreciating the way Jessica's face was relaxing as she sipped her cocoa and watched the ocean. "I'd be glad— Huh?"

Jessica smirked without even turning to look at him. She clearly knew what effect she was having on him…and didn't seem to mind, which gave him a sliver of hope.

He did his best to force his attention back to Monica.

"Well, her Scottish pub makes her the biggest restaurateur in town. Cal Jr. at The Blackbird Bakery is handling the cake, but I'm desperate for the food. You'll take care of that for us?"

"For how many?" He'd been invited, he was fairly sure of that. Living back in Eagle Cove a calendar had become less and less meaningful. Five days working for the Judge, the rest of his time, social or cooking, was typically fluid on a daily or even hourly basis. "How elaborate? And for how many?"

Mrs. Baxter looked ever so innocent as she said, "Nothing fancy. It's an afternoon wedding, so just a friendly sit-down dinner right here." She waved a hand to indicate the grounds of the old Victorian. The large grassy yard sprawled out to the sea cliff.

Jessica's eye roll told him one degree of the trouble he was in.

"And I think we only invited twenty or thirty."

Fewer than he'd fed last night so—

Jessica practically snorted her cocoa with laughter and gave herself a coughing fit that had her mother suddenly solicitous.

"How many invitations did you sent out, Mom?"

She shrugged delicately, she was a softer version of Jessica. Was that time or was Jessica merely a more sharply edged person? Jessica cut a far sharper picture in the world.

"Thirty."

"Anyone turn you down?"

"Just your aunt, but since Gina is going to be my maid of honor again, I know she's just teasing."

Jessica turned to face him. "That's thirty *families*. Plus, knowing Mom, anyone else she happened to be chatting with or sold a house to or…"

Greg blinked hard. Mrs. Baxter wouldn't have thought a thing about inviting people. She had an outgoing warmth that made her one of his favorite people in town completely aside from her role as Jessica's mother.

"Maybe you should start with an elk," Jessica teased him.

"Too bad the gray whales are done migrating," he shot back. Every spring they shrimped their way up the coast, returning each fall. But this was July and he knew nothing about cooking whale anyway.

"Or tourists. No one would ever miss a couple of tourists."

"And I thought I was the one getting ghoulish," Greg grimaced.

"No tourists," Monica Baxter stated as if it was a rule rather than disgust. "They're the ones who buy weekend residences and hire out my Ralph for day-trip fishing. I refuse to cut into the family businesses for this."

Greg laughed as Jessica looked at her mother as if she'd grown a second head. He leaned back in his chair and enjoyed the moment. He knew exactly what she was feeling. It was just three years ago that he'd come home and discovered that his mother and father were not the people he'd thought they were—they were better. He recalled the shock of seeing Judge Slater so shattered by the loss of his artist wife. That's why he'd stayed in town and his father had appreciated it, not that either would ever say a word on the subject of course. Apparently Jessica had been unaware of her mother's sense of humor.

"I'll do it, Mrs. Baxter. We'll need a better estimate of how many I'm cooking for, but I'll come up with a couple of menu ideas for you."

"Oh you sweetheart. I always knew you were a good boy," she leapt to her feet and offered him a hug and a kiss on the forehead. Then she turned to her daughter, "Well, I have a house-showing out at the Carson place in half an hour, so I have to run along. Natalya and Gina went out with Ralph to spend a day together on the water, so you have the run of the place."

And in an instant he was alone with Jessica Baxter and a sudden awkward silence descended on the porch.

Greg nursed his coffee but couldn't think of a thing to do to break the silence. He'd abandoned her on the beach last night. Yelled at her about him being an idiot. Great. He'd found a way to be insulting to both of them. And if he sat here like a dumb mute much longer, he'd blow any chance of—

"You were going for a run?"

He looked up to see Jessica was still gazing out at the ocean. "I was."

"Give me a minute," and she rose to head indoors, leaving him to contemplate her undressed look as she walked away, and the rumpled quilt now abandoned on the porch swing.

In moments she was back. The shorts were no longer, but they were now visible as the loose nightshirt had been replaced by a form-clinging t-shirt in fire engine red that declared: *Journalist!* in a headline bold font followed by: *Mess with me and I'll spell your name wrong.* The t-shirt wasn't made out of the thickest material.

"Go ahead, spell it wrong, please!" Greg teased her. "I'd bet anything that it would be completely worth it."

Her laugh was merry as she rested one of those long legs on the porch rail and began stretching out. A last sip of the coffee did nothing to jog his brain to life. He knew how to talk to pretty women, had earned himself a bit of a reputation for how easily he could sweep up a tourist. He just didn't know what to say to Jessica Baxter and she absolutely knew it. He retreated to the kitchen to rinse out his mug and buy himself a little space.

# # #

By the first hundred yards along the beach they were pushing the pace enough that no spare breath remained for conversation which was fine with Jessica.

When they reached the docks at the two-mile mark and moved up onto the streets, she picked up the pace another notch. Her long legs could run most guys into the ground, but Greg not only kept up, but began pushing her. Up Beach Way, she saw his shoes and socks still on the porch of The Puffin Diner, looking as if their owner had been teleported out without his footwear.

What the hell, Slater? Was that really what she'd said about such a fine meal?

No, that's what she'd said about a man with a boyhood crush on her. Well, she'd only be here for one week, then she'd be safely gone. They couldn't cause *too* much trouble in such a short time.

They ran out to where the town tapered down into the single road. At the final intersection before it headed up into the Coast Range she turned them onto Gull Way. It looped along the backside of Eagle Cove, making the longest possible running route.

In high school, it had been a straight 10K: Aunt Gina's down the beach, through the heart of the town, up and down the short hard hills of Gull Way, cut back along Shearwater Lane and out LBB Lane. She'd usually started the loop at the high school on Shearwater, but had run it from Aunt Gina's often enough that it was like coming home to run the loop.

Out on Shearwater, Greg slowed and waved at someone.

Jessica waved out of habit, but almost stumbled as she took in the image. It was a double-wide manufactured home, just where she'd pictured Greg, Dawn, and a passel of kids. But the home was clearly well tended with a cheery paint job and colorful hollyhocks. In front of a large add-on garage were parked a newer minivan and a beater pickup. But what made her stumble was that Vincent, Dawn, and the twins were all working together in the garage workshop on a beautiful-looking bookcase. Not at all the sort of place she'd pictured them ending up. It looked…cozy.

She started paying more attention to the town they ran through. Growing up here, it had all turned into the blur of "home." Being gone, that memory had turned into rundown and sad. There were still those types; "white trash" places piled with mossed-over trailers, salvaged materials that would never be used, and lopsided picnic tables. But there were also the crisp lawns that marked retired military and the toy-strewn yards of new toddlers.

She almost commented on it to Greg, but then they hit the top of LBB Lane and now he kicked it up a gear.

Two miles to go, he was clearly trying to run her into the ground. Well, that wasn't going to happen. Not to Jessica Baxter. Especially not on her home turf.

"Elmer," she gasped out, finding it easier than she'd like to sound completely winded.

Greg nodded. That was their finish line.

Elmer was the massive Douglas fir that ruled over Aunt Gina's property. It had been there when the house was built and would probably still be there when the Victorian fell down from old age. Elmer was a two-hundred foot-tall old growth, easily seven feet through the trunk.

She let her stride open up and shifted her focus from the houses onto the end goal, calling up the techniques that had gotten her to the regionals if not all-state.

Pictured it in her mind's eye. Not the stretch of road ahead of them or the stiff climb as the road ascended from beach to top of bluff. Not the point where tar shifted to gravel on the final stretch. Jessica firmly planted the image in her head of arriving at Elmer far enough ahead of Greg Slater that there would be no question that she hadn't only beat him with some final sprint; she'd crushed him.

Chicago's biggest hill was the freeway bridge over the river, but she'd balanced out that lack of elevation with longer miles along the lake's edge which was totally paying off at the moment. Running was one of the few things she'd taken with her when she left Eagle Cove and the chance to run here was such a pleasure that it made her feel like she was flying.

Greg did his best, he really did, but she could see that he had nothing left to dredge up when she kicked into her final sprint as they passed the Slater's. She felt a dozen feet tall as she crossed Gina's lawn in first place.

She didn't so much reach Elmer first, but rather ran square into his massive trunk braking with only the last step. Jessica tagged the tree and then splayed herself out against the rough bark so that she didn't collapse to the ground. Maybe she wasn't in quite as good practice as she thought. A moment later Greg did the same—he must have found reserves somewhere to finish just a single step behind her. Good thing she'd been trained to never look back. That simple action might have cost her the race.

Rich pine and dusty bark overwhelmed her own sweat. Salt dripped down to sting her eyes and flavored her lips when she licked them.

"Damn. Jessica," Greg gasped out. "But you. Can. Really run. Damn!"

Laughter bubbled up and almost choked her as she still couldn't get enough air.

As soon as they could stand without Elmer's support, they began walking circles around the tree, shaking out legs, and walking it off.

"C'mon," Jessica nodded toward the kitchen.

They staggered up the broad front steps together—knees loose, bumping shoulders and laughing as they went. It was a good moment, one Jessica realized that she'd treasure for a long time.

# # #

Greg had a whole lot of thoughts as they leaned back against opposite counters in the Lamont B&B kitchen, guzzling monstrous glasses of orange juice. The kitchen had been utterly modernized, in ways that made it look traditionally old. Black appliances, walnut cupboards with brass handles, and dark granite counters. The hardwood oak floor was finished and sealed. The indirect and discreet lighting was unneeded as the sun was currently streaming in through the eastern windows lighting Jessica's hair as she leaned by the sink. She was positively a shining beacon offset by the lush warmth of the décor.

He was no longer thinking of the woman with the amazing body. Well, not only. He was also seeing the woman who never bowed to a challenge but instead grabbed it with both fists and her teeth besides. Someone who understood that there was nothing as funny in this world as people, especially the ones you cared most about. He was telling her about the courtship between Dawn and Vincent with full DVD-extras commentary: Vincent hadn't stood a chance, but Dawn had made him think that he was the one making all the "right" moves.

"He only figured out how to court her because she told him when to ask her out for dinner. When the first kiss was okay. Half the time she fed the tips and cues through me without me realizing it either. She led him like a puppy dog each step of the way," Greg tipped his head side to side like a dog just trying to figure out what was happening to him.

Jessica's merriment had her snapping her fingers and slapping her hand against her bare thigh, calling out, "Here, boy. Here, boy."

Eight days. Don't do anything stupid…at least not too stupid, one side of him admonished.

To hell with that! Greg's other half answered. He had a bad habit of listening to that side and he decided that this time wasn't going to be an exception.

He set down his glass, circled three times in place like an excited puppy dog with big galumphing steps, moving closer to Jessica with each turn as she laughed and kept clapping her hand.

At the end of the last circle, he stepped between her spread feet, leaned in and kissed her.

Fifty-fifty he was going to earn a slap. Forty out of the remaining fifty he was going to get shoved back on his ass hard. Ten percent odds seemed pretty good for a chance to finally kiss Jessica Baxter.

He caught her mid-laugh.

She felt better in his arms than he'd ever dreamed. Her slender frame let him wrap his arms right around her back. Her lips tasted of salt sweat and sweet orange juice, and her laugh continued for a moment as a vibration that shifted into a thoughtful, *Hmmm.*

Greg didn't feel thoughtful at all. He was wholly focused on the way the length of their bodies pressed together, of her arms slipping around his neck as the kiss deepened. Unable to resist, he pressed himself against her. His hands slid up and down her back appreciating the curves and shapes. No bra strap obstructed his investigation, not that Jessica's build particularly called for one. She was sleekly perfect.

Her kiss was shredding his recipe for how this might possibly go. The blood pounded in his head as he held her closer.

Then he felt a cold trickle, almost icy cold.

Right on the top of his head.

He tried to pull back to see what it was, but Jessica had her arm locked tightly about his neck…one arm. She even wrapped one of those infinitely long legs around his waist which was very distracting.

But the cold trickle continued. Then the first ice cube bounced into his hair as chilly orange juice spilled down his forehead and stung his eyes.

"Hey!" (which came out more as "Mgrph!") He tried again to escape and she held him even tighter.

That laugh was back in her kiss, but she didn't release him.

Well, two could play that game.

No they couldn't. His glass was over on the opposite counter.

Fine. Then he'd play it for all it was worth.

He tipped her back against the counter just enough that the juice was trickling down both their cheeks and spilling between them rather than running down his back.

The laughter slipped back out of her kiss—damn, there'd never been anything like kissing Jessica Baxter. Once the flow of orange juice and ice cubes stopped, she fumbled for a moment to set the empty glass on the counter and then both hands grabbed onto him.

He brushed a hand upward, appreciating every muscle. Relishing the softness of her hair and the curve of her ear. Then, as casually as he could, he collected the ice cubes that had perched in his hair rather than tumbling to the floor. With just as smooth a move, he ran his knuckles smoothly down her cheek, her neck, and managed to slip the ice cubes inside her shirt collar.

This time it was her turn to struggle and squirm and his to laugh into their kiss. He kept their bodies close enough that the ice cubes couldn't slip past her breasts.

When she finally freed a fist and pounded its side against his shoulder, he backed off. With a judicious grab on his retreat, he managed to yank forward her shorts just as the remainder of the ice cubes slithered out the bottom of her t-shirt.

Jessica yelped as the ice cubes slipped into her underwear.

Life was so good. "Paybacks are hell, aren't they, Ms. Baxter?" He dropped back to lean against the counter—where he'd been standing before all of this had started—and admire the view. Orange juice dripped from her bangs and face. It plastered her already clinging t-shirt tightly to her figure, now forming little more than a sheer overlay. Very admirable.

She reached down, pulling aside her shorts and shaking a leg. The slender ice chips that remained, shattered with soft pops as they hit the kitchen floor.

"You have no idea about paybacks, Mr. Slater." Jessica glared across the kitchen at him, "You have no idea at all…yet."

"Nope!" he agreed as pleasantly as possible. "No idea at all. But I can't wait to find out."

She headed toward him, her sneakers splashing a little on the few puddles of orange juice that hadn't soaked into their clothes. Jessica was moving like a cat on the prowl, swinging hips, eyes locked on his. He didn't know if he could move, but he didn't want to so it didn't matter; this was far too much fun.

But he wasn't paying close enough attention to what else was going on and realized it too late.

She leaned up against him and for a brief moment he once more tasted the orange juice on her lips. But before he could cradle her back against him, she was easing away.

Easing away and—

She'd grabbed his own glass of iced orange juice from where he'd set it on the counter behind him. She didn't trickle it atop his head this time…she dumped it! The cold was breathtaking.

He managed to grab her as she danced back—her bright laugh filling the room—but lost his balance, his sneakers turned to ice skates on the suddenly slick hardwood floor.

In moments he was down, but he didn't lose his grip…not until she landed atop him.

His breath escaped him in a whoosh as her hip crashed into his gut.

Straddled over him, she looked down at him with a puzzled expression.

Any thoughts about what it might mean were washed from his brain as she lay down upon him and kissed them away.

She was right. Paybacks were hell; his kind of hell.

# # #

Once they'd cleaned up the kitchen, and they'd showered—separately—Jessica sent Greg trotting home in his rinsed-out clothes and squishy sneakers. He could have stayed in a towel while his clothes tumble-dried, but she didn't mention that option. He'd be right back, as she'd promised to make brunch for him, but she wasn't ready to face a naked Greg clothed only in a bath towel.

During the run, she'd worked on her mental man-list a bit. She wasn't an intentional tally-keeper and it definitely wasn't well thought out, but every now and then she'd run into something and add it to her list. Most items she learned about men landed solidly in her no-way-in-hell category. Some fell into her wouldn't-that-be-nice-even-if-she-was-never-gonna-find-it category. Very few items fell into the required category.

She started the bacon and scrounged some smoked salmon, then thin sliced a local white cheddar and found some crumbly gorgonzola to balance it.

Greg had added "fellow runner" to her preferred list. A good sense of humor had been on the required short-list since forever, but she nudged it up a few notches in his honor. And fun! When had she lost sight of the importance of fun? Dad had a decent sense of the ridiculous but Mom's first divorce had kicked the crap out of Jessica's taking joy in it. She couldn't remember the last time she'd had as much fun as wrestling with Greg among the orange juice. Had she ever? There was another thought she wasn't ready for.

Some flour tortillas and she mashed an avocado—making poor man's guacamole with a scoop of store-bought salsa and a sprinkle of cayenne.

Someone to hold her as if she was more special than she knew she actually was would be a great bonus. And the way that man could kiss…

"You're awfully intense when you cook."

Jessica yelped in surprise. Greg stood mere inches off her elbow.

"I like that in a woman." He looked just as good in jeans and a button-down shirt as he had in running shorts and a t-shirt.

"I bet you're one of those guys who likes anything that's female." She cracked four eggs into a bowl, added a splash of cream, some shaved cilantro, and salt and pepper, then began beating it while the pan heated.

"Give me some credit," Greg complained.

"Like what?"

"Well, having a preference for beautiful ones who are cooking for me. I'm a chef; cooking women are a major turn on."

Jessica dumped the beaten mixture into the pan and intentionally nearly rammed him with the fork and bowl as she turned to put it in the sink. She definitely needed a few more feet of space. Greg Slater *was* a major turn on, even if she didn't want him to be.

She stirred the eggs with a spatula, crumbling in the bacon and smoked salmon. It was going to end up tasting very smoky. Jessica spotted a lime in a bowl on the table and squeezed it to drizzle through her fingers to catch any seeds. Then she folded in the cheese. She zapped the tortillas for twenty seconds in the microwave, spread a line of guacamole then sour cream down their centers, and dumped the egg-cheese-salmon-bacon mixture in. With a quick flip it folded into a breakfast burrito.

She dropped a tub of yogurt and a bowl of blueberries on the breakfast nook counter that faced toward the woods then sat on one of the stools.

"Brunch!" She announced.

"Where's the orange juice?" Greg complained rather than complimenting her food.

"Careful, or you'll be wearing what little is left." She made a fake shudder, could still feel the stickiness that hadn't seemed to come out of her hair in the shower. "Not sure I could face it right now."

"Me either now that you mention it. Two glasses of milk coming up," he went to the refrigerator and served them both.

He bit down on the burrito and looked at her strangely.

"What? You're supposed to compliment your hostess' food, even when it doesn't deserve it. Where are you manners, Slater?"

"My manners—"

"Clearly don't include not talking with your mouth full."

"—are being blown away by your cooking. I figured you'd turned into some helpless city girl whose idea of cooking is choosing which takeout to get."

"Trust me, I wish I was. But I'm broke," and she sure as hell hadn't meant to let *that* slip out.

"I…hmmm," Greg thought while he chewed, thankfully swallowing before continuing. "Last night. You mentioned that, but it didn't make sense. I read your writing, you're really good.

And you're in a half dozen markets which…" he tapered off and then concentrated on his breakfast burrito.

"You've read my writing."

He nodded.

"But I write mostly for the Chicago market."

He nodded again, spooning up a small bowl of yogurt and blueberries as if it was the most important thing in the world.

"The *Chicago Tribune* has a paywall."

"Maybe I subscribe," he was adding more yogurt, building such a mound that she finally stopped him by resting her hand on his.

He froze in mid-scoop, but his hands were warm and strong beneath her fingertips. She pulled back but the sensation didn't go away.

"Maybe I subscribe to every market that an online search turns up with you in it." He dished half of what he'd served himself over into her bowl.

Jessica rested her chin on her palm and her elbow on the counter. It put her closer to Greg than she'd anticipated, but she felt no need to pull back. "I'm going to repeat a question, but try not to be mad."

He shrugged an easy acceptance.

"What the hell, Slater?"

"I know," at least he had the decency to grimace. "Kind of cyberstalkerish."

"Kind of," she was torn between agreeing and being touched.

"It's become almost a joke, a joke on myself. Look, Jessica," he turned those dark brown eyes on her, "I know I'm an odd person. I know that I'm at least as bizarre as Vincent or Dawn or the twins will be some day. I'm holding a torch for someone I never expected to see again. And all those fantasies?"

"What?" she asked despite her better instincts.

"They aren't a touch on the real woman who can write the way you do, cook a damn fine breakfast burrito, or feel so amazing in my arms." No matter how odd he might have thought he was, Greg didn't look aside for a single moment of his confession.

Jessica knew it was a mistake even as she reached out to take his hand.

"I'm implying nothing beyond now," she managed a whisper.

His brow furrowed briefly as she rose and gently tugged him to his feet. Feeling more overeager seventeen than her usual coastal twelve or Chicagoan thirty-two, she led him away from their half-eaten meal and up the carpeted, creaking stairs. She closed and latched the door behind them.

Jessica ignored Xena the Warrior Princess' smile of approval from her place on the back of the door.

When Greg laid her down on the bed, the only sound in the room was the ocean surf moving the sand infinitely back and forth far below the open window streaming with sunlight. Sometimes clichés—something she assiduously avoided in her writing—had their place. Jessica decided this was one of those as she gave herself to the moment.

Chapter 5

Saturday Afternoon

W ell," *Jessica's voice was* pleasantly husky and smooth as a slow-pouring honey, "that was fun."

Fun? "Sure was." She was the queen of understatement.

Greg now knew what heaven felt like. It felt exactly like this. The warm ocean breeze rippling over the woman wrapped against him. Only a thin sheet and a glow of well-earned satisfaction covered them. If kissing Jessica while swimming in orange juice had been merely wonderful, making love to her had been fantastic. It hadn't been a merry wrestle like the kitchen. Instead it had been a surprisingly tender voyage of discovery.

Not that there was a coy bone in her body. She'd given herself thoroughly, abandoning herself to the act. He had done his best to return the favor and between them there hadn't been a single word, but there'd been no mistaking the shudders of pleasure that had shaken both of them. His pulse had long since recovered, but his head was still spinning pleasantly at the wonder of it all.

Her fingers traced lightly back and forth over his chest and he allowed his own fingertips to linger on her arm. This he could get used to, very used to. And one way to make sure that happened, was by being considerate.

"We need calories. Someone, brilliantly I might add, interrupted our breakfast. I'm feeling seriously depleted." She slid a hand down and cupped him, it elicited only a marginal external response, though it made his breath catch and his eyes would have crossed had they been open.

"Uh-huh," was her only observation.

"So," he managed, "I shall sally forth and recover the rest of our breakfast."

"Sally? Like in a shining knight?"

"*C'est moi!* Breakfast in bed sound good?"

"Mmm," she agreed, but she didn't release him. Instead she burrowed her face into his chest and they started all over again. Thank god he'd taken the risk and brought a strip of protection back with him. Next time he's bring several strips, long ones.

When they were finally finished, again, she lay back and groaned. "Food. I need food."

Food? He lay fully upon her with his face buried in the pillow beside her head. He needed to never move again. *And what kind of a shining knight does that make you?*

He forced himself to action until he was standing, a feat he'd thought beyond him. Reluctantly, he pulled the sheet over Jessica, but her soft sigh made him feel noble and he'd return in moments.

# # #

Jessica did manage to force an eye open to watch Greg's naked behind heading out the door. It was a very nice one that went just fine with the rest of his body. The muscles she'd dug her hands into as she'd struggled to pull him closer, gave way to a strong back and nice shoulders. They weren't broad and powerful, they were just very, very nice.

No, the powerful part of Greg Slater was his hands. They had the finesse of a chef and the strength of one as well. He'd found ways to make her—

She heard a microwave cycle on in the distance.

He was even reheating their breakfast.

Then in quick succession she heard: the slap of the screen door, a very male yelp, and feet pounding up the stairs.

Greg burst through the door in a state of wild panic, slammed it behind him, and leaned back against it. Xena looked over his shoulder, apparently approving of this as well. Greg now offered her a very nice chance to admire the front view, if she hadn't been laughing quite so hard.

"Who?" She choked out.

His eyes merely bulged in panic.

He spotted his clothes and dove for them as somewhere in the background a microwave beeped four times calling for attention.

He was mostly dressed by the time steps sounded up the stairs.

At the soft knock, he grabbed a stray sock, one of hers, and bolted into the bathroom.

"Yes?" Jessica managed to call out without choking herself. She sat up and pulled the sheet up under her arms so that she was decent.

"I was coming by to see if you wanted to go out for lunch, dear." Her mother spoke through the still-closed door. "Apparently not. But someone left your tray in the kitchen, dear. I brought it up for you."

"Come on in."

There was a brief hesitation before she did. After a quick glance around the room she smiled, a little more wickedly than Jessica would have credited Monica Baxter being capable of.

Jessica pointed at the bathroom door, and Mom's smile only grew bigger. She didn't react at all to Jessica's complete *dishabille* nor the stray clothes scattered across the floor that showed she had been a little distracted by other concerns on her arrival.

Her mother set the tray on Natalya's bed, winked, and headed back out the door.

Jessica really needed to rethink her relationship with Mom. No lectures. No scowl. Quite the opposite in fact.

With the door almost closed, she stuck her head back into the room and called out, "It's safe to come out now, Greg."

"Thank you, Mrs. Baxter," sounded through the bathroom door.

Then she was gone. Jessica could get to really like her mom in addition to loving her. To avoid laughing again at poor Greg, Jessica reached out and snagged her burrito. She had time for several bites and some leisurely chewing before a very red-faced Greg Slater emerged from his bolthole.

"Some shining knight you are." He still held her sock.

"Give me a break, Baxter," he sat on Natalya's bed and picked up his own burrito, still uncertain quite what to do with the sock in his other hand.

"Of course, you did moon my mom," hopefully he'd been facing the microwave which was on the opposite side of the kitchen from the door. "I suppose that counts for something." Jessica didn't like the fact that she didn't like Greg sitting so far away, as if two feet of difference should matter. Normally she liked her men to keep their distance; it made casual sex so much more…casual.

"I'd rather face a dragon," he mumbled as he bit down on his reheated breakfast.

"I'll find one for you. Now come back to bed."

He eyed the closed door over his shoulder, then shook his head.

Jessica released the sheet from under her arms and let it slide back down into her lap.

Greg's eyes widened, without even tracking down. Then he smiled, tossed her sock over his shoulder and, taking one last bite of his burrito, began undressing all over again.

Gods but there were times she loved men.

Chapter 6

Sunday Night

G*reg sat in the* Baxter's kitchen, as modern as the Lamont B&B's was classic. It was also one of the most efficient layouts he'd ever seen in a home kitchen, clearly Ralph Baxter's doing. However, Ralph wasn't here at the moment and Mrs. Baxter was making his head spin almost as badly as her daughter did.

For the last day and a half, he and Jessica had rarely been more than an arm's length apart. And now, when he could really use her help, she and Natalya had gone off to do "girl things." They'd actually said it that way, "Girl things." What the hell were those? Well, the itch between his shoulder blades told him the topic of their conversation even if he didn't know where they were or what they were doing.

Instead he was sitting with Monica Baxter, her sister Gina Lamont, and a moderately battered yellow pad on which he'd been scribbling down menu ideas for next weekend's wedding.

Page one through four had been the seafood draft. The three of them had worked out the details of the courses and the flavor progression, shifting dishes to match the bride's tastes and her sister's practical bent from running the Lamont B&B. Then Ralph Baxter had wandered through with a set of socket wrenches in his hands. Just in passing he'd remarked, "Be nice if it wasn't fish. Spend all the damn day out on the boat with fish."

And he'd been gone again.

Greg had sighed and folded the pages under, starting again with a French menu.

They were most of the way through when Ralph Baxter came back in carrying about a third of an outboard engine.

"Not on my kitchen table, Ralph Baxter," Mrs. Baxter declared moments before greasy machinery met bright oak.

"Not your table until you marry me again, honey, but I take your point. Wasn't thinking. I'll get some newspaper and do it in the living room." Then he glanced over Greg's shoulder.

Greg gave him long enough to absorb the first page, then flipped to the second one. He didn't have a chance to turn any of the next four pages before Ralph spoke again.

"Thought you wanted something light, honey. That's some serious cuisine Greg's got going there." And he lugged the engine through the arch into the living room. His fiancé scrambled to her feet and after grabbing a garbage bag and a couple of issues of the Newport newspaper—at a few dozen pages it was the thickest one on the coast—raced after her husband.

"That man," she sighed as she returned to the kitchen.

Taking his cue, Greg folded the pages of the French menu under. Well, at least he had some good ideas for the next couple Irregular Fridays at The Puffin.

"Mediterranean?" he suggested.

Gina Lamont's eyes shifted from him, to her sister, to the bright tick-tick-tick sound of the socket wrench coming from the living room. "Yes, but Greg…if Ralph comes back in, don't let him see the menu."

Greg considered for a second, then scrawled a one-page menu in large letters before turning it for the sisters to see.

Burgers and beer!

They all shared a laugh, then he flipped the page over and started working on an Italian four-course meal. It pieced together quickly.

Jessica would like this meal. A Tuscan white bean soup, which was a little heavy for the season, but he could offset that with seasonal greens and a tomato base. A crab-artichoke ravioli would follow served with a side of arugula and a basil-infused vinaigrette.

He knew he was on a roll by how few additions Gina was making this time.

And then…

He pictured Jessica eating this meal. It would be delicate, light…it was a lover's meal. A meal he might spend a day making just for the two of them. Or perhaps a Couple's-only Night at The Puffin. It wasn't a meal of celebration, it was a meal of wooing and love.

It was an absolute certainty that's what was happening to him. Yes, his fantasies about her had been so wrong; Jessica Baxter was no longer eighteen and leaving for college. But the grown woman was a revelation of her own in attitude and style.

He'd enjoyed their quiet walks and talks on the beach as much as he had when they tumbled together and lost all of their words. He couldn't imagine ever getting tired of either side of Jessica.

"Greg?"

"Hmm? Oh," his attention slowly returned to the women planning a wedding celebration.

" 'Oh'?" Gina winked at her sister. "I know that look."

"Counting the days, Sister," Monica agreed.

Jessica had told him of her mother's peculiar no-sex-outside-of-marriage rule. She had scoffed, but Greg had rather liked it. While he wouldn't trade back a single second of the time he'd spent in Jessica's arms these last few days, a part of him wished that they had waited. Wouldn't that have been a glorious wedding night?

A true celebration.

A celebration.

He slowly flipped back a few pages to the note he'd scrawled pending Ralph Baxter's return to the room.

Burgers and Brew!

"The exclamation point says it all."

"What does it say?" Monica leaned in.

"A celebration," he looked up at her. "Which do you want, Mrs. Baxter? A lover's meal or a celebration?"

"Duh!" Gina chimed in. "Fourth time's the charm!"

Monica looked down at the three words in front of him for a long moment. And then she smiled a long, slow smile that her daughter had inherited straight down the matrilineal line and only used when she was particularly pleased with something.

He flipped to a fresh page and began writing and talking at the same time.

"Sage and rosemary Dungeness crab-stuffed mushrooms. Sliders of Marv's grass-fed beef with Eric's brie-and-bleu cheese melted in the center served between thin slices of baguette garlic toast—light on the garlic because it's a wedding. Maybe topped with a paper-thin slice of prosciutto. Tiny-potato, skin-on French fries with a balsamic-ketchup drizzle."

Greg could feel the excitement growing at the table.

This was how Jessica made him feel. He'd spent far too much of his life struggling to make fine food. Last Friday's halibut service had been the pinnacle of that progression. It had been true fine dining in a coastal diner.

But that's not who he was, or at least not all of it.

He was the man who could make Dawn laugh even in the moment when she was ready to execute Vincent. He loved teasing the twins until they were lost in fits of merry giggles. Entertaining the Judge's sleepy breakfast customers was always a bright start to his day.

"I love making her laugh." Then Greg froze. He hadn't meant to say that aloud. Especially not to Jessica's mother and aunt.

They were both looking at him with sympathy, but it was a male voice that spoke first.

"She needs that," Ralph Baxter, his hands smeared with grease, including a couple of stripes on his face, stood in the doorway to the living room. "Lord alone knows she had little enough training in doing that. Most serious girl there ever was. I was good in school, but I was never driven the way she is."

Greg pictured an orange-juice soaked woman laughing with delight in the Lamont kitchen and wondered. It seemed such a natural part of her in that moment, but it was true that he hadn't seen much of that particular aspect of the woman before or since.

"I'll do what I can, Ralph."

"Easy enough to see that you love her as much as I love my gal," he stepped the rest of the way into the kitchen and leaned down to kiss Monica on top of the head. Then he checked the back of his knuckles before smoothing them down over her hair.

"You get grease in my hair, Ralph Baxter..." she left the threat hanging.

Ralph just grinned at him over Monica's head, still brushing her with the clean back of his hand.

Greg couldn't help but return his smile.

"I don't think he heard what you said," Gina told her sometimes brother-in-law. Her radiant smile left no doubt about what she was referring to.

She was wrong. Greg had heard it loud and clear.

Easy enough to see that you love her as much as I love my gal.

Greg just didn't see any point in arguing with the truth.

#

Girl things.

Today's girl things included going out to visit Becky Billings BlueBird Brewery and sample the beer; which had turned into sampling a lot of beer.

Bluebird had been Becky's nickname ever since Jessica had tagged her with it in kindergarten during a chorus practice. Bluebird could sing circles around the rest of them even at five. Jessica was quite proud that the nickname had stuck and been transferred into the company name. Becky had grown up to be one of those women who made short and curvy look like a serious amount of fun. Her thick brown hair fell straight down past her shoulders and the top of her head barely matched Jessica's chin. She was also strong from physical labor and it showed in all the best ways.

"I'm selling from Tillamook to Coos Bay and I just opened into Eugene. Time to hire some help I guess."

"Make sure he's a cute one," Natalya chimed in.

Jessica nodded her agreement and then wished she'd been a little less emphatic in doing so. Becky's brewery swirled and wobbled for a moment after she stopped moving her head. The big steel tanks and pipes visible through the large window behind the tasting bar were momentarily unstable.

The tasting room itself was rustically elegant. When Becky's dad retired, she'd sold the cattle to a farmer up near the Tillamook Cheese Factory, rented out most of the fields for hay, and converted the barn to her one true love, the brewing of beer. She'd started with root beer in junior high and never looked back.

The tasting room itself had been the old calf barn—a friendly, cozy space. Remnants of stalls along the back wall divided stacked cases of bottled beer into different sections, probably so they didn't fight with each other.

At the moment Jessica was too comfortable to watch beer bottles heaving caps at one another in pitched battle. She turned her attention back to the counter once more. It was lined with small glasses. They had been drinking four-ounce tasters; the problem was that Becky's beers were so…tasty.

Jessica started giggling.

"What?"

"We're testing Becky's tasty tiny tasters."

"You're drunk," Becky announced.

Jessica started to nod but thought better of it.

"She's also getting happy sex," Natalya told Becky. "As if she wasn't obnoxious enough to begin with."

"Excellent. Anyone we know?"

"Greg," Jessica battled with an incipient hiccup and won, "Slater."

"Oooo," Becky made it a long, salacious noise.

"It's not like that," Jessica protested and picked up a tiny glass of Hummingbird Ale—a bright, cheerfully fizzy beer.

"It's totally like that!" Natalya leaned against the bar a little harder. It was a classic long bar: heavy wood, a line of stools on her and Natya's side, a row of taps on Becky's side, with the windows to the darkened brewery behind. The room was dim and quiet on a Sunday evening, but it was easy to picture a party here—a crowd of happy tourists plucking cases of their favorite brew from the stacks scattered in their stalls. She resisted giggling at the on-going alliteration.

"Should have the wedding here," then maybe she'd spend it drunk and not have to face being second bridesmaid to her own mother. Aunt Gina had been the first bridesmaid every time. *Ha!* And she'd been there every time as well, even if the first time she'd been in her mother's womb instead of in a dress.

"Your wedding?"

Jessica scowled at Natalya, "No! Mom's. Duh! That's never going to happen with me."

"Not even to the handsome Greg Slater?"

"Not even."

"She's just using him for sex," Natalya confided somewhere in Becky's direction.

Her words were slurring as well and she looked distinctly blurry.

"It shows," Becky agreed.

"What shows?"

Neither of them answered her. Instead they both gave her "significant" looks. She wasn't that drunk.

"Nuh-uh! Nothing different about this girl, nothing changed by Greg or his hot body."

"I knew it!" Natalya crowed.

"Don't care what you *know*," Jessica tried to make little air quotes with her fingers but ended up with something closer to air Cheerios. Or perhaps air Fruit Loops. "Marriage is not something you'll ever catch this girl doing."

Again the two "significant" looks.

"It's not like marriage means anything." Nothing but layers of paper stuck to the breezeway door. Divorce, marriage, what was the difference? "Not a thing," she insisted.

She rested her chin on her crossed arms and stared at the mug that Becky set inches from her nose.

"What's that?" It was dark. And it was steaming. "Are you trying to serve me hot beer? That's disgusting, Bluebird Becky B."

"Nope, it's coffee."

Jessica burped, keeping it as soft as she could. "Rather it was beer."

"She'd rather it was Greg Slater," Natalya stated like some goddamn know-it-all.

"And who is getting into *your* knickers, Natya?" It was the best retaliation she had at the moment. It didn't help that her best friend was right. Greg was acting like a drug on her system, one that there was no way to get enough of and she didn't like that at all.

"Knickers. Getting awfully arcane there, Baxter." Then Natalya sighed sadly. "No one is getting in them at the moment."

"I know the feeling," Becky's sigh matched Natalya's.

The perfect chance for revenge, "Greg is getting into mine every chance he has." She resisted adding a *Nyah, nyah, nyah!*

"We already know that," Becky growled.

Aw, what the hell. She gave them her best, "Nyah! Nyah! Nyah!"

"Maybe we should steal him from her. I don't think she appreciates what she has."

"Sure, Natya. Fine. Whatever," Jessica would have waved a dismissive hand, but her head felt too heavy to raise off her arms. She settled for a finger flick like brushing away dust, but no one saw that because she did it on the wrong side. That was the problem with crossed arms, it made everything confusing—like she didn't have enough of that already.

Except she didn't like the idea of giving up Greg. Not even a little. She…liked Greg. Not just in bed either, where he was proving to possess an endless amount of resourcefulness and creativity with a very nice helping of stamina when it really counted. She really did like Greg out of bed a lot. She actually could picture him more easily with his clothes on and a laugh on his lips than she could naked with her against his lips.

There were times she could imagine being with him for more than her eight days in Eagle Cove—

Whoa! Not a chance that was going to happen! She shook it off.

She needed to make sure that didn't happen because it just wouldn't do. Her life was enough of a mess right now. Between her career, her mother's wedding, her return to Eagle Cove… Greg was definitely one too many things to deal with.

She squinted to focus her eyes on Becky and Natalya. They were reminiscing about some of their high school sweethearts. There was laughter and lightness. She felt like an orange-juice soaked rag: damp and starting to smell a little…off. They were clean and fresh because they were unencumbered. But she was trapped between great sex with a nice guy versus some chance of dealing with everything else going on in her life. It was a tough choice, but she knew what she had to do. Time to take action.

Jessica pushed herself upright, shoved aside the coffee, and knocked back a four-ounce tiny taster of Strawberry Stout.

Fumbling out her cell phone, she was surprised to find Greg had been added to her contact list. When had that happened? How was he suddenly so far into her life?

She punched the "call" icon on her third try.

It was ringing.

"Hello there, pretty lady," Greg's voice was warm, smooth, an intimate caress.

"Hi, honey," her mom called from somewhere in the background. Okay, so much for the intimacy of their moment.

"Hi, Greg."

Natalya and Becky, caught in mid-sentence, both turned to look at her.

"We're just sitting here and planning the wedding dinner. What can I do for you?" There was something funny in his tone.

"You aren't talking about the wedding. You're talking about me," Jessica could feel the blood rushing from her brain to heat her face.

"Guilty."

"With my mother!" The horror of it rose up and tried to choke her.

"And your aunt and father."

Jessica couldn't breathe. Her heart was racing faster and faster. Just her and Greg she could deal with. Adding on Natalya's and Becky's teasing only made it feel like old home week; they were her inner circle ever since preschool days.

Her parents and aunt took the story to a whole other level. She didn't need to be an interview journalist to know where this was heading and it was scaring the crap out of her. *A good journalist never shows their emotion, but instead reflects the emotion that will lead the interviewee to say more.*

"Are you still there?" Greg's question told her that she was blowing this.

"Uh-huh," was the best response she could dredge up despite her vaunted emotional control.

"Is there a reason you called?"

"I called?" Oh, right. *She* had called *him*. To…oh!… "Yes," she tried to clear her throat and instead the hiccup she'd fought down before snuck back up. "I—"

I what…?

"I just wanted to tell you…" There had been a reason she'd felt the urgent need to call Greg right away. It was… "that we're through." Natalya and Becky gasped in surprise. "It's been great fun, Greg. But enough is enough. Let's not sp—" the hiccup finally escaped in a cliché-sized *Hic!* "—oil it. Great se—*hex*. Se-*hex* has been great. Was great. One of those things. Thanks. Bye."

She ended the call even as Greg shouted something in a panicked tone. Jessica looked around the bar top for something to celebrate with.

The phone in her hand rang and vibrated almost making her drop it.

Greg.

She stared at the display through three rings until she could be sure that she was hitting the off button rather than the answer one. For good measure, she turned the phone off and dropped it on the bar. Then she found another tiny glass of she couldn't tell which beer. At least it wasn't black and steaming.

Jessica raised it in a toast to her friends, "Too free-*he*-dom!" Free-he-dom! Perfect! She'd drink to that.

When it didn't look like they were going to join in, she downed the beer in two swallows and thunked the glass back on the wooden bar top.

"I forgot," Becky studied her, "that you're the stupid drunk of this crowd. Thank god I'm the happy one."

"Stupid?" Natalya was practically yelling. "Idiotic!" She'd always been the rational drunk—which really shouldn't be allowed when drinking was going on.

"Shush!" Jessica waved a hand for them both to calm down. "It makesh per-*her*-fect sense," which was almost as good as Free-*he*-dom. "Though I will mi-*hish* that body. Did I tell you that Greg Sl-*hate*-ter has a wonderful body?"

"We don't want to hear it," Natalya groaned.

"Knows just what to do-*hoo* with it too."

"I'm going to call Greg back and you're going to apologize."

"Don't you dare!" Jessica clutched her shut-off phone to her chest and hoped that Natalya didn't have his number.

"I want to hear about his body," Becky protested. "Give us all of the details. Now that you've dumped him and are in the no-guy zone with the rest of us, we should at least get some fun details."

Dumped him? Had she just dumped him…right, she had.

It was all for the best.

Too bad it felt like the worst. Which was fine. Everything else in her life was feeling that way too and now Greg fit right in.

# # #

For lack of anywhere better to be, Greg had spent the evening and well into the night sitting quietly on the front porch of the half-filled Lamont B&B. As it was obvious over the phone that Jessica was drunk, or well on her way there, he'd scouted around town. But Jessica wasn't at the Bobbin' Red Robin Tavern or the Brass Plover Pub. He'd even checked to see if she'd decided to party on the afterdeck of her father's fishing boat. Greg ignored the fear as he rushed there that she'd had too much, fallen overboard in the middle of their conversation, and been washed out with the tide, because that was just a little too psychotic even for him. The boat rested dark and quiet at dock.

Natalya was also nowhere to be found which made him feel a little better. It was always better to go on a bender with a friend.

Imagining Jessica drunk had passed some of the time. Was she a giggler? Hard to imagine. Thankfully, Jessica as a morose drunk was even harder to picture—though he'd met plenty of those back in his restaurant days; that type was practically epidemic in professional kitchens.

He checked his watch. Two a.m. He had to get up in three hours to help the Judge with breakfast service, but he knew there was no sleep waiting for him if he gave up his vigil.

There was an honesty to the occasional drunk that worried him. Chronic drunks were often chronic liars—first of all to themselves. But the occasional drunk would lose their inhibitions and say things they never should have said in the first place no matter how true they were—a problem Greg had thoroughly demonstrated a few times in high school. That was how Vincent knew about the true depths of Greg's infatuation with Jessica Baxter.

Well, he was stone cold sober—and fairly cold as well sitting out here on the porch all night, waiting for a crazy woman who had broken up with him over the phone.

It couldn't be real. It just couldn't. He wouldn't let it be. He'd never fought for a woman before, but this time he'd—

A brightness filtered into the trees. He double-checked his watch, 2:03 (three whole minutes later than the last time he'd checked). So, it wasn't sunrise.

The light flickered and brightened: car headlights approaching from a distance, stray beams scattering through the trees. It took a curiously long time for the car to appear. When it finally did, he understood why. It was moving very slowly. Becky Billings' van finally crunched to a stop on the gravel driveway close beside the front steps. Damn it! He'd never thought of going out to Becky's brewery.

Greg scrambled down the stairs.

The passenger door opened and Natalya climbed out.

Before he could do anything about it, Natalya stepped into his arms, gave him a very sound kiss, and then snuggled up against him.

"Hmmm," she let out a long hum of delight that he could feel rippling down her body. "Jess is right. You have a very nice body, Mr. Slater." She squirmed more tightly against him and giggled at his body's reaction. She was warm, soft, and clearly quite drunk.

"Keep your voice down, lots of people are sleeping here. Uh, where's Jessica?"

"Spoilsport," Natalya mumbled but didn't move away.

For lack of any better tactic, he scooped her up into his arms, her head never moving from his shoulder.

Becky had climbed out of the driver's side. "Has she passed out yet?" Her speech wasn't exactly clear either which explained the painfully slow and careful driving.

"Close enough," Greg traded smiles with her. But awake enough to supercharge his body. "Where's the other one?"

"She's out cold," Becky hooked a thumb toward the back of the van. "I'll watch over her while you dump Natalya in bed."

Greg nodded and entered the B&B as quietly as he could. The main staircase was barely wide enough and each creak had him wincing, but by twisting sideways at the turns, he managed to carry Natalya up to her room. He lay her on the bed and pulled off only her shoes before covering her. Undressing a beautiful drunken woman was not going to be on the list of things he'd done this night and would have to explain in the morning.

He went back down and circled to the rear of the van. Becky had the door open and a dome light revealed Jessica sprawled on a horse blanket. She wore a flirty summer dress, that had ridden very high up her legs.

"She was very emphatic about us not calling you," Becky cracked a smile that made him feel better than anything else had this evening. "Sorry about that."

"It's okay."

Becky turned and sat on the edge of the van's deck, facing the night.

As there was no way to move the sleeping Jessica while Becky sat there, Greg turned and sat beside her, shoulder to shoulder. Actually, she was short enough that it was more his shoulder to her ear. They remained there a long time before Becky spoke.

"She's very fond of you, Greg."

"Thank god." He'd prefer more than fond, but after all of his worries this night he'd take any tidbit he was offered.

"More than that…"

"Double thank god."

"…but she's got some shit going on. Not my place to say, not that she said all that much. Jess always did play her cards close. But you and I go back a ways and I want you to know that I'm rooting for you."

"You always were a good friend." And she had been. He ran a hand down her back and kissed her atop the head. They'd dated for a few months when he'd first returned to Eagle Cove. It had been fun, but it hadn't turned into anything serious. She'd become a good friend since, one he counted on for far more than her fine hand at brewing.

"We talked a lot and some things are obvious—at least to Natalya and I if not to Jessica. So, I'm going to say this with the love I have for both of you: don't let her slip away. She's going to try very, very hard. Don't let her, Greg."

"I won't." Not a chance. No one knew about the patience and tenacity necessary to achieve a goal like being a chef.

Becky looked up at him.

"What?"

"I've had just enough to drink to say this. There are times I wish things had worked out between us. Even back three years ago you were something; you're way better now. Don't get all cocky, but don't forget it either." Then she pulled his head down and gave him a long, hard kiss. It was enough to remember all of the things that had been good between them without interfering with what was amazing between he and Jessica.

There was a soft, "Hey!" from inside the van.

He could feel Becky's grin before she broke the kiss. "You said you dumped him and he's fair game now," she said to Jessica without releasing her arms from around his neck.

"Oh. Right. Sure. Go ahead," each word from Jessica slid closer and closer to a sleepy mumble.

He and Becky both turned in time to see her once again collapse into sleep.

"It's a good thing that I love her so much, Greg Slater, or you wouldn't stand a chance."

"Woman as good as you, maybe I wouldn't want one." And while he knew it wasn't quite true for either of them, it would have been nice if it had been.

She pecked him lightly on the lips before letting go, "Let's get your girlfriend out of my van. What you do with her after that is up to you."

He held her in place a moment longer. "Whatever man you end up with Becky, if he forgets for a moment how goddamn lucky he is, just let me know. I'll come over and pound some sense into his thick skull."

Becky giggled, "Very kind, Mr. Slater. And an absurdly male offer."

He shrugged; it probably was.

"Besides, can you see me needing help to drive common sense into a man's head?"

"Nope, I bet you can handle that just fine, but my 'absurdly male' offer stands."

Then they stood and he scooped Jessica into his arms. Unlike Natalya who'd been all clingy and sexy, Jessica was as lively as a sack of potatoes.

"Lucky bitch," Becky whispered in her friend's ear and then kissed her on the temple. "Shoo! I've got to get home to my cold and lonely bed." And she was creeping the van out the driveway before Greg reached the porch.

He was half tempted to carry Jessica back to his house; it was just the next one toward town on LBB Lane. At least there he could curl up against her for a few hours before he had to go to work. But that probably wasn't the best choice. First, she'd probably wake alone while he was at work. Also, ultimately, he had to straighten out the fact that she'd broken up with him before he made any assumptions.

Greg crept up the stairs and lay Jessica on the bed. He removed her shoes and did his best not to think about how cute she looked in the flowered summer dress by what moonlight was wandering in the window. Maybe she'd wear it for him to dinner one night and he could take it off her then. Actually, there were liberties he was willing to take with her for her comfort that he wasn't willing to do for Natalya.

He slipped off the dress, doing his best not to admire the body he was only starting to learn about. He could spend a lifetime exploring it and never be bored. Again, all she wore beneath the dress were panties—these were covered in cheery miniature sunflowers. He turned to dig in the dresser for a nightshirt, then thought better of it. The woman might be fussy about a man digging through her underthings.

Then he had an idea. Greg peeled off his own t-shirt, slipped it over Jessica's head, worked her limp arms through armholes, and tucked her under the covers. There was a brief reaction to his goodnight kiss, but brief was the key word there; a pleased hum in the back of her throat and then a slide back into drunken sleep.

Natalya hadn't wiggled so much as a finger since he'd tucked her under.

He turned out the light and crept out of the house. Without his shirt, it was a cold trot home, but it would be totally worth it.

Greg just wished that he could be there to see her face when she did wake up.

Chapter 7

Monday

A pillow slapped into Jessica's face and her headache exploded to life.

"What the hell?" She barely managed to fend off the next blow.

"You're such a bitch," Natalya dropped the pillow back on her bed with a thump and groaned.

"Why am I a bitch?" Jessica managed to crack open one eye to look at her cousin sitting on the edge of her bed with her head hanging down in her hands.

"First, you break up with Greg."

Oh crap! She had, hadn't she.

"Do you really still think that was smart?"

She did. She didn't have to like it, but it was the right choice. He was being an Eagle Cove chef and she was returning to Chicago in just five days. Everything was getting too close and intense when she already knew how it was going to end.

"Second, you just *had* to tell us quite how amazing he is in bed."

"I didn't," please tell her she hadn't. But Jessica could remember snippets of doing just that. She pulled her own pillow over her face to hide her embarrassment. "I did," she mumbled into its depths.

"You did. In thoroughly decadent detail and we were drunk enough to listen to every sordid detail," Natalya's voice shuddered as if she'd never purge the images. "And then third, the part that makes you a total bitch, you got all drunk and miserable and sad like the little puppy dog you are. That made me feel as if someone should keep you company with your drinking." Natalya groaned again. "How was I supposed to know just how much you'd drink?"

The way Jessica's head felt, she'd didn't want to know the answer to that question. She raised a corner of her pillow and caught sight of Sigourney Weaver aiming a massive rifle at a slobbering alien. She looked ready to conquer the universe and Jessica doubted she could conquer a piece of toast at the moment.

Natalya flopped back onto her mattress, "I swear, cousin or not, I'm going to kill you if I ever recover." She still wore the clothes she'd had on last night, though they were now much the worse for wear from sleeping in them.

"Um," the last thing she really remembered was Becky's tasting bar and a shockingly long line of small but very empty glasses. "How did we get here?"

"Don't know," Natalya flopped back on her bed and dragged her own pillow back over her face to shield against the sunlight slipping through the *Harry Potter* curtains featuring a very ticked off Hermione Granger wielding her shining wand.

Maybe she knew a magic spell for hangovers. *Curiatus!* No, that was too much like the *cruciatus* curse presently throttling her skull from the inside.

"I remember kissing someone," Natalya posed it as half statement, half question.

"It wasn't me, was it?"

"No. Male. Very male. Good kisser too."

"I'm a good kisser, too," though why she was arguing about it was beyond her. "But I'm not male." Jessica didn't remember kissing anyone. She wished that she had. Someone who could help her purge Greg Slater from her system. Even thinking of him made her feel all mushy inside and that absolutely would not do.

There was a soft knock on the door.

"Go away. There's no one alive in here," Jessica called out then really wished she hadn't as her headache explored previously undiscovered levels of awfulitude.

"I have coffee and hot chocolate," a male voice answered through the door.

"Coffee!" Natalya moaned from beneath her pillow.

Hot chocolate. Right at the moment, she would kill for some.

"And aspirin," the muffled voice called out again.

"Ohh!" Natalya moaned with delight.

"Enter oh god of the day," Jessica called out. "Just do it softly."

It wasn't until he was opening the door that Jessica realized who the voice belonged to. She really didn't want to see Greg, especially not after breaking up with him over the phone—a rather abrupt pronouncement that had not been kind. But it was too late on both accounts: the breakup and the permission to enter. He was already through the door, smiling in at them.

"It is noon. I thought you might want to get up."

Natalya still mumbled from beneath her pillow. "Noon. Sun at brightest. Must hide."

"Cof-fee," Greg teased and Natalya emerged slowly and took the mug Greg was holding out.

Jessica continued to watch him with the one eye she'd uncovered. She'd rather hide, but she did enjoy looking at him.

"Here," he held out a mug of steaming hot chocolate with a dozen tiny marshmallows bobbing merrily on the surface.

Her father had told his little girl that marshmallows were signs of pirate treasure lying below the surface and each must be swallowed up to reach the prize. She'd always drunk her cocoa that way ever since. He'd told the truth. At the bottom of every mug lurked a treasure of extra-rich chocolate that settled so warm in her stomach.

She struggled upright, shoving and pushing until she could lean against the headboard, a carved relief of King Kong. Natalya's was of Fay Wray, the woman who had brought about the downfall of the great beast. The carving was just deep enough to make a good backscratcher. Her nerve endings were universally fried and appreciated the gentle massage.

Greg was grinning at her as if she was naked and had once again just dropped the sheet to expose her breasts and entice him back into bed. But she wasn't. She was wearing a t-shirt, a nice roomy one that wouldn't show anything.

Natalya turned a bloodshot glance in her direction and then nearly snorted her coffee.

"What?" Jessica looked down. This wasn't one of her t-shirts. In fact, the last thing she remembered wearing was the dress presently spread over the back of a child-sized captain's chair that belonged on the bridge of a miniature *Enterprise*. No, *Star Trek Voyager*. Jessica recalled a stuffed Captain Janeway doll was perched in the seat, even though she was presently giving orders from behind flowered cotton.

It took Jessica a few tries to find the hem of the t-shirt and hold it out far enough that she could read it upside down.

All men are created equal…then the very best become chefs.
Greg's.

She pulled out the collar and peeked down her front. No bra, though she hadn't been wearing one with the dress either, so she couldn't really blame that on him. Her panties were still in place. Jessica looked back up at Greg's smiling face.

"Cad!" She put some heat behind it as a tease, but he took it seriously—a flash of pain that slid across his features then vanished. She didn't know quite how to take it back.

"Proud to be," his cheery response showed just how decent he was as he dug deep to offset Jessica-the-bitch.

Her alter ego mixed with her headache in a very not-cheery way.

Natalya looked down at her own rumpled blouse and skirt, "Not enough of a cad." She looked at Jessica, "Stingy of you not to share, Cousin."

Then a funny look crossed Greg's face and a blush. Jessica had never met a man who blushed so easily.

"I think, Cousin," Jessica called over to Natalya but didn't look away from Greg's dark eyes. "I think I have found the male who kissed you."

"Wha—" Natalya hesitated. "Hmm," a thoughtful sound. "Maybe."

"Actually she kissed me," Greg mumbled then smiled at Natalya. "Quite thoroughly."

Jessica winked at her cousin, "Told you he was a good kisser."

"Hmmm," this time there was more the sound of pleasure than thoughtfulness in Natalya's tone.

"Though," Jessica stirred up the best glare she could and aimed it at him, "I seem to recall you kissing Becky too. But not me."

"*You're* the one who broke up with *me*."

And in that instant, even the marginal joy of teasing Natalya went out of the conversation.

She could see Greg's hurt at her reaction, but she couldn't hide it. Even in full journalist mode, Jessica could no longer hide what she was thinking from Greg—a skill that had served her well with previous lovers.

"Can we talk about this later?" She plucked at the t-shirt which suddenly felt so tight and constricting that it threatened to choke her. She couldn't seem to get any air.

He froze for a long moment, then spun to his feet and was almost out the door before she could think to call after him.

"Greg!"

"What?" It was more a snarl of pain than a question.

"I wasn't saying that to avoid talking about it. Just give me long enough to shower and change."

He didn't turn and his shoulders didn't relax as he remained braced in the doorway. "You aren't denying it either," his voice was rough.

She wasn't. "Please?"

And after another long moment, he growled, "I'll be on the beach." Then he was gone.

Natalya looked at her.

"No. I don't know what I'm doing," Jessica admitted. "I wouldn't mind some brilliant advice."

Natalya just shook her head. "Sorry, Cousin. I've got nothing this morning. You'd be better off asking one of them," she waved at the science fiction heroines who populated the room.

She looked at the triptych of framed posters hanging along the far wall: Katniss Everdeen of *The Hunger Games* and Neytiri in her *Avatar* blue separated by Natalie Portman as Isabel in *Your Highness*. All were pictured with bow and arrow fully drawn, their eyes clearly focused on the target. They were all such strong, fierce women. She was just a lonely struggling journalist. Not a lot of help there.

She hurried into the shower not sure how long Greg's patience would last. Jessica left the hot chocolate cooling on her nightstand, its marshmallows now melted into a congealed mess that was slowly sinking into the muddy liquid. No treasure there today.

# # #

Greg had somehow convinced himself last night that Jessica hadn't really meant it, which only proved what an idiot he was.

When he'd put his t-shirt on her last night, it *hadn't* been some attempt to mark his territory, conscious or otherwise.

And then he'd seen her final expression change. Jessica's face was such a subtle one. Like a great actress, there was no single identifiable change, yet her face had completely shifted without moving at all. It had happened while she was tugging at his t-shirt as if she was going to rip off the vile thing whether or not it would leave her naked.

What it all translated to was that she'd meant every word on the phone last night, drunk or not.

How had she greeted him with such seeming pleasure on his entrance this morning and then so cruelly dashed his hopes? He dropped onto the sand, scowled at some tourist's dog that came trotting over for a sniff, and barely resisted yelling at its owner for not keeping it to heel. The beach was dog heaven and they should run free here. There were waves to dive in, endless seagulls to chase but never catch, and high-lobbed tennis balls flicked from their owner's launchers to arc down the beach or out into the waves. But why should a goddamn dog be having such a good time when he was—

"Hi." Jessica came up beside him.

How deep was the black hole that he'd been moping in that she'd had time to clean up and come find him? A pretty deep one.

She shifted from bare foot to bare foot, but showed no signs of settling.

With a sigh he patted the sand beside him, "Sit down. I won't bite." Maybe if he'd been friendly with the dog, it might have bit her for him.

Jessica hesitated several very long moments before sitting. She wore a wide-brimmed straw hat with a blue strip of gauze tied about the crown; it fluttered in the soft breeze as if it was trying to reach out to him—the only part of her that was. She stared straight out to sea with her legs pulled up tight against her chest. She looked pale, even by her fair-skinned standards.

Much to his surprise, she was still wearing the oversized chef's shirt.

"Why don't you take that damn thing off?"

"I was going to. I did to shower. But I…" she inspected him closely from behind her dark shades, then shrugged when he gave no sign. "But I didn't want to."

"Whereas taking me off and casting me aside, that was as easy as a phone call." The depth of his anger surprised him. Last night he'd been planning Monica and Ralph Baxter's wedding, but without any realization on his part, he'd also been planning his and Jessica's at some unknown future date. He didn't notice that until it was taken away.

Shit!

He'd thought Vincent was the goofball, Dawn the smart one, and him somewhere safely toward the Dawn end of the spectrum. Turned out he was the idiot of the gang. Perfect!

"No," Jessica's soft voice barely intruded on his thoughts. "It wasn't easy. And the way I did it wasn't kind, but I still think it was kindness."

"You're going to have to explain that, Baxter. Use simple words. I'm just a dumb chef, not some brilliant, straight-A school valedictorian."

She dug her fingers into the sand and let it trickle back through her fine fingers and dribble over her bare feet.

Fingers that could make him feel so—*Shut up, Slater!*

"Your infatuation with me—"

"I'm done with that, Jessica. I get it but I'm goddamn done with it! Now, I'm—" he bit down on his tongue to stop himself. He wasn't going to spread the carcass of his sad past out on the sand for the gulls to pick over.

"I was going to say that your infatuation with me ended up starting something wonderful."

So, shutting up had been a good choice. Would have been nice if he'd done it sooner, but it was too late to help that.

"This isn't about you. It's about me."

"That's a pretty damned pat answer. We are—were in a relationship. As in two people, not just you. How is it *not* about me?" His voice kept rising and he couldn't stop it. He also still couldn't bring himself to look at her.

"You're right. I'm sorry."

In his peripheral vision he could see her hand reaching out, but then she pulled it back.

"My life is in freefall. It's already more than I can deal with. You're wonderful, Greg. Really. I barely know you, but I strongly suspect that you may be the best man I've ever been with."

He liked the way "best" sounded. He badly wanted to be Jessica Baxter's "best." Greg dug up a fistful of sand himself, but when he started dribbling it out it immediately began filling his sneakers. Dusting off his hands only spilled sand into this pant cuffs. If that was "best," maybe she should keep looking.

"You're handsome, smart, and funny. You cook like a goddamn god and having sex with you is more fun than a girl could ask for. More than *I* ever thought to ask for." She said the last line more to herself than to him, but he couldn't leave it alone.

He reached out and took one of her hands. He wondered if Natalya had alerted her mother and they were both atop the cliff looking down at them through binoculars. A glance down the beach revealed his father on one of his post-cooking constitutionals, but he was too far down the beach to matter. Tourists who hadn't brought picnics had headed into town for lunch, so this end of the beach was relatively quiet.

She was rubbing her thumb back and forth across the back of his knuckles, looking down at their joined hands so that her hat hid her face. He'd rather keep his mouth shut, which had been working well so far, but he had the feeling that if he didn't say something, Jessica might never speak again. He remembered what Becky had said last night, or rather this morning: *Don't let her slip away. She's going to try very, very hard. Don't let her, Greg.*

"Okay." If he didn't speak, he was afraid that neither of them would. "I'm going to steal a question from a very smart person."

He didn't continue until she looked up at him. He reached out and slipped off her sunglasses so that he could see her shaded eyes—those brilliant blue eyes that missed nothing, yet he had so enjoyed making sightless with passion.

"So, if this really isn't about me, then my question is this. What the hell, Baxter?"

# # #

Jessica wanted to hide. She wanted her sunglasses back to hide her bloodshot eyes from the glaring sand. The typical bank of dense summer fog was lurking a few miles offshore, obscuring the horizon but leaving the beach bright and clear, so no help there either. She wanted to look away from the beautiful man whose brown eyes somehow saw past her defenses, yet didn't turn away from the mess that poured out of her. And most of all she didn't want him to stop holding her hand because it felt like the only thing that was keeping her from shattering into a thousand pieces.

"This is Monday, Greg. My parents' fourth wedding is on Saturday," as if there could be a more meaningless act. But, if it made them happy, more power to them. "On Sunday morning Natalya drops me at the Portland airport and I'll be in Chicago that night."

"Uh-huh."

She could use something more useful than a male grunt as a guidepost, but she guessed it was all the help she deserved at the moment.

"We had a couple of great days." A couple of utterly *amazing* days and a night in between them that she wouldn't forget for a long time.

The small guest house on the Judge's property where Greg lived was her idea of perfection. It was a grand Victorian shrunk to the perfect scale for a small family who thought that being in each other's way was a good thing. It was too easy to imagine such things when she was there. It was one of the reasons she'd scared up Natalya and gone to Becky's. Part of the reason had been to get the old gang back together, but part of it was so that she didn't crawl into that house with Greg Slater as if she'd never leave—when she knew full well that she would have to.

"I grew up with parents who were in love, but can barely tolerate living in the same house. Mom has this whole separate residence through that breezeway. When Dad started building it, it was supposed to be an office for her business on one side and a workshop for Dad on the other. His workshop became a bedroom, den, and kitchen as well—then Mom doesn't understand why his projects end up being done all over the house. And Dad built it for her as if it was okay that his wife didn't live with him part of the time. Or lived with him, but—" she didn't know what.

She struggled to her feet, couldn't tolerate sitting still any longer. Greg didn't let go of her hand and their connection pulled him to his feet as well. They began walking down the beach, like lovers holding hands, not like two people trying to resolve a fight before one of them left to never come back…and after the way this week was going, she was *never* coming back to Eagle Cove.

They walked down to the sand hard-packed by the retreating tide. It was the main thoroughfare up and down the beach. Sitting in the deep sand higher on the beach, they'd been left to themselves. Here they were having to constantly shift their path to avoid clumps of kelp, gaggles of children, and couples who actually might be lovers walking along together. The locals had all hit the beach hours ago, jogging or walking the sand while the tourists were still abed. Now it was midday and she didn't recognize anyone—not a soul to distract her from the hard task of explaining herself to Greg.

"I don't want that. I don't want marriage. I'm open to living with a guy, the right guy." She saw Greg's questioning glance. "My roommate is single and straight. *She* has a cat. I've never had a male *roommate.*"

"I've had female roommates," a fact that Jessica wished he'd kept to himself. "But that's all they were. We were broke sous chefs trying to make ends meet while we served our time as kitchen slaves."

"But when does it end? The kitchen slave part of it." She'd served her time. And her career was more down the hole than it had been five years earlier.

"You always keep learning."

She got that.

"But your industry is getting kicked out from under you," Greg added before she could say something nasty.

"I seem to have noticed that. No suggestions for the sad journalist with a blistering hangover who just kicked a handsome good guy out of her bed?"

He gave her the laugh she'd been looking for and she felt better. "Not a thing."

"Thanks a bunch."

"But I'll give it some thought."

Jessica stopped and squinted at Greg. He actually would give it thought. "I was right. You *are* a good man, Greg Slater."

"Shh!" he glanced up and down the beach quickly. "It's my first time and now you're going to jinx me."

She couldn't help herself, she kissed him.

It was supposed to be a friendly peck of thanks, but somehow she melted back against him. Wrapped her arms around him hard and held on as if she were clinging for dear life.

When at some point—maybe after the tide had turned or the world had spun on its axis a few times or something—she was no longer kissing him but instead lay against him with her head upon his shoulder, she knew she wasn't going to stay away from him while she remained in Eagle Cove.

"If this is how you do it," Greg nuzzled her ear as he spoke, "let me just say that you're really lousy at this whole breaking up thing. I'm liking your way of making it up though."

"You're a guy. You just want make-up sex."

"I *am* a guy, so of course I do. Doesn't mean I'm crass enough to ask for it though. Especially not with the shape you're in."

"What's wrong with my shape?"

And he groaned at the trap he'd just sprung but just held her tighter. Jessica lay against Greg's chest for another timeless amount of time. It was a place she didn't have to think, could just be. People wandered by. Some laughing, some chatting. A pair of surfers went by in dripping wetsuits from tackling the short, hard surf just out from the long facade of The Sleepy Owl Hotel. One of them said, "Get a room, you two," as he walked by.

Jessica could think of many things she should do. Go spend some time with Mom or Dad. Catch up with friends she hadn't seen in years and might never again. Get online and see if there were any developing long-lead stories that she could do research on and maybe track down a few inside contacts before she got back. But they would all require that she let go of Greg and she didn't like the idea of that. Not at all.

Get a room had stuck in her head.

They hadn't walked all that far past Greg's house.

"I could maybe be talked into a little make-up sex."

"You're joking," Greg made it a statement.

But… "Actually, I wasn't."

"But that means…what?" Greg didn't pull her away from his chest to look at her, but instead just kept holding her as if this was the normal state of being for them.

Jessica gave it some thought and finally had to admit, "I don't know. I'm lost here. I broke up with you and I wish I hadn't, but I don't know what that means either. However, having make-up sex sounds better than not having it and it's all I have to go on."

"That almost made sense," Greg teased her a little before his tone went more serious. "You scared the crap out of me, Jessica."

She nodded against his shoulder, "I know. I'm sorry. Scared myself too." Scared at just how deep her attachment to Greg had become and how quickly.

"So, no-commitment make-up sex?"

Against she nodded, hoping it was the right choice. "You'll have to be gentle though, I feel as if bits and pieces of me are constantly on the verge of passing out again."

"I'll be very gentle."

And he was. He was very gentle…and *very* thorough. And for one of the first times in her life, Jessica did nothing but lie on his bed and let the sun shining in over the ocean wash across her as a man made her feel utterly amazing.

Chapter 8

Tuesday

*S**he emerges.*"

"Eat shit, Natalya." Okay, maybe she had lost Monday afternoon to Greg making lovely sex with her. And maybe, after they'd both slept for a while, she'd spent a fair portion of the night doing her best to give back as good as she'd gotten.

And maybe there'd been a quick round of wake-up sex during breakfast—kitchens seemed to fire up Greg's imagination; *hello, he's a chef. no big surprise.* It had made an incredible finish to the make-up sex. And she was going to pretend that it wasn't only people who were dating or were couples who had make-up sex. After he headed to the restaurant, she'd slept another few hours. They hadn't spoken, not much. Which was just as well because as good as her body felt, her brain was still mostly mush.

"Let's see," Natalya took a piece of paper off the nightstand. "Your mom won the pool."

"What pool?" Jessica started digging in the drawers for a fresh t-shirt. All Greg had were chef ones and for some reason she'd ended up wearing the fuzzy face of the Muppet's Swedish Chef declaring "Kiss the Chef!" Jessica had kissed Greg—very much had—which made it seem appropriate when she had pulled it on. But now it conveyed a degree of coupleness that was uncomfortable with. She felt like a story element out of its proper context.

"Well, you didn't give us time to make a pool on how long until you got back together. Instead we took bets on how long your make-up sex would last."

Jessica stopped with a t-shirt in her hands that said: *I'm a journalist! To save time let's just assume that I'm never wrong.* She shoved that one hard into the bottom of the drawer and found an old Northwestern University t-shirt to wear instead. Once properly protected from complete ridicule by being clothed as herself once more, she turned back to face her grinning cousin.

"My mom bet on how long Greg and I would have sex?"

"She nailed it within twenty minutes. Aunt Gina thought that you'd try to slip in before dawn so that you didn't technically spend the night. Bluebird was always a romantic and bet you'd play house for another day."

Jessica flopped onto her unused bed, face down into the pillow. The coolness of the not-slept-on Wonder Woman linens only emphasized her heated cheeks. So much for not feeling farcical. "What was your bet?"

"You don't want to know," Natalya sounded like she was gloating.

Jessica sat up enough to reach out and grab the piece of paper before Natalya could stop her. Across the top in bold letters she'd written: *When will J. reemerge? ($5 to enter.)* There were a dozen names with dates and times. Her dad even. And names she didn't even recognize that might be guests at the B&B.

Maybe she could get a flight back to Chicago tonight. Too bad the antipode of Eagle Cove lay somewhere deep in the Indian Ocean or she'd go there to be as far from here as possible. NASA really needed to get the whole flights-to-Mars things going…now.

Down by Natalya's name, rather than a day or time, she'd simply written: *Never!*

"What the hell, cousin?"

Natalya shrugged. "I'm on your side. And I can always hope."

Jessica planted her face back into the Wonder Woman pillow.

# # #

The high whine of Vincent's table saw made speech mostly impossible this afternoon and Greg was thankful for it.

He'd started the morning feeling high as a kite. The thoughtlessly complete welcome he found in Jessica's arms had blurred the last twenty-four hours into a single, very pleasant memory with a thousand little highlights. The possibility that he might have the chance to wake up day after day to discover Jessica wrapped about him had been a vision of the future that overwhelmed him. The sex had been fantastic, but it was the holding and companionship that were rapidly becoming his favorite aspects of their relationship. He'd never imagined her as the kind of woman who snuggled, but she absolutely was.

There had been so little time for talking. He had the sneaking suspicion that was the important part and he'd better be careful not to neglect it.

Throughout the Judge's breakfast service, he'd pondered that more and more.

He'd promised to think about her problem but then proceeded to not be able to focus. The trouble with thinking about it was that he knew nothing about journalism. He was one of those people who actually knew almost nothing about the news. Other than restaurant reviews, if Jessica Baxter didn't write about it—and her niche was special interest not world news—then he knew squat about it.

He fetched boards for Vincent from the stack and caught them as they came off the saw with a nice forty-five degree bevel down their length. A quick flip and another cut for a double bevel. Goggles and heavy earmuffs made for safety but prevented most conversation.

It was a real problem talking with Jessica at all when the other option was getting his hands on her.

"Are you covered for all of this lumber if the client flakes?" Greg shouted in between cuts. There was thousands of dollars of hardwood stacked here and weekenders were notoriously unreliable customers.

"They paid half of labor up front and all materials on their account, not mine. Forty percent on installation and the last ten percent on acceptance."

Greg shot a thumb's up and went for another piece of oak. Clearly Dawn had negotiated the contract no matter how unhappy she was about what it was doing to her family life this summer.

Actually, he and Jessica had talked plenty in between bouts of sex, but it was all about the past and the Judge's offer to bankroll the start of his restaurant. None of it was about the subject of her future…a topic she seemed to be avoiding.

Did journalism work like the Kriegson's contract ? Half up front? He'd wager not. Especially not for a freelancer like Jessica. She'd started full-time at the *Chicago Tribune,* but had become a stringer since then. He'd tracked down her writing in a dozen different places, but even that seemed to be tapering off.

A chef who had a restaurant paid his employees first, his vendors second, landlord third, and then prayed there was enough to pay himself. The good restaurants could always do that. Feeding people was steady work. *Focus on your people and the menu,* he'd been told by any number of chefs, *then the rest works out.*

"Yo!" Vincent shouted at him and Greg got back in motion. Staring at the lumber wasn't helping Vincent.

None of that would be of any help to Jessica either—just staring at the problem was useless. But there had to be some way that she could get paid up front, even half.

He picked up another length of 1x6 oak and delivered it to Vincent.

# # #

"Since when do moms have nerves?" Jessica asked and the whole group started laughing.

Knitting was a serious business in Eagle Cove and anyone who could get away met at the Lamont B&B's verandah Tuesday and Friday afternoons, or in the period-decorated parlor when the weather was less friendly.

Her mom was all in a fuss over wedding details that clearly had nothing to do with the details and everything to do with a barely controlled state of panic.

"Just wait until it's your wedding, young lady. Then I dare you to be calm about it."

"Double dare you!" Natalya jumped right in.

It was lucky that Becky was out doing deliveries today. Jessica wasn't in the mood to face a triple dare.

Tiffany stopped knitting on her Fair Isle leggings long enough to hold up three fingers. *Triple dare! Crap!* At least Tiffany's name hadn't been on the sign-up sheet for the Jessica-and-Greg betting pool. Jessica sighed, she'd probably only missed it because she hadn't come down out of her woods while the pool was running. Tiffany returned to her knitting and Jessica did her best to follow her example.

"Your mother is right, dear," Mrs. Winslow patted Jessica's shoulder. "I was a complete wreck. Of course I only did it the one time." She aimed an arch look at Jessica's mom who appeared completely oblivious to it.

"It's hard to imagine you being a complete wreck." Mrs. Winslow was more of a Rock of Gibraltar type of woman.

"Oh, it turned out well enough, but on the day of, I would have taken a one-way ticket right back into Saigon even if the war had not been over by then." She'd come to Eagle Cove almost straight from reporting on the Vietnam War and married an older retired-Navy man who taught junior high math. Her two boys had been finishing high school by the time Jessica and Natalya had reached Mrs. Winslow's class and Jessica only barely remembered them from occasional visits home.

She let the conversation move on without her as she focused on her knitting. A stripe of butterscotch gold and another of light woodland green. She had plenty of scarves and had traded in her long straight needles for four shorter double-pointed ones to start again, because you could never have too many pairs of thick warm socks. Once she'd started knitting again it had come back easily. Anyone could make a pair of socks—though she might need some help remembering how to turn the heel. She wasn't too proud to ask; she'd just sneak a look in Aunt Gina's *Vogue Knitting* book the next time no one was around. It had meant pulling out a dozen rows of scarf but a woman was allowed to change her mind, wasn't she?

Change her mind.

Like her break-up, make-up, wake-up with Greg Slater. She froze as she recognized the pattern of her last few days. Please god, someone tell her that she wasn't like her mother.

She glanced at Monica Baxter. Having given control of the wedding meal to Greg, she was now worrying about the rehearsal dinner. *Just a judge's civil service wedding on the B&B's lawn. Get a grip, Mom.* Gina had offered to do a big BBQ for the dinner, but because Greg had gourmet sliders on the main wedding menu, Mom wanted to change everything Aunt Gina had planned for the rehearsal.

Jessica turned back to her scarf-turned-socks and focused as hard as she could. Chatting was usually one of the joys of knitting. Except when doing a tricky section or detailed lace work, her hands could run along mostly on autopilot allowing for other enjoyments like conversation. But now she was trying to avoid both the conversation and her own thoughts and the sock was not providing the haven she so needed. She was out of the gold ribbing, which had at least offered an alternating knit-purl for a minor distraction, but now it was just a dozen rows of knitting green in a circle without even a purl in sight.

Change her mind.

Why was that thought sticking around? Like maybe she should change her mind about being a journalist.

She dropped a stitch, then saw that was because she'd dropped one on the prior row. She tried to pick up the dropped stitch in the prior row and only managed to cascade the loss back another row.

Jessica stilled her hands, rested the whole thing very calmly onto her lap, but wasn't paying attention to the needles. One of them had only a single stitch on it—you never let go of a needle in such a state. There wasn't enough yarn friction to hold it in place. The needle slipped out, dropping yet another stitch in the current row, and fell onto the porch without making a sound, which was odd. There should have been a bright *Ping!* drawing all attention her way. Leaning over, she couldn't spot where it had fallen.

She glanced at Tiffany, who of course again hadn't missed anything. She pointed straight down. Jessica looked again by her feet, then Tiffany pointed downward more emphatically. Jessica eyed the dark gap in the old porch decking—too narrow for even a stiletto heel, but big enough for a single knitting needle if it fell perfectly.

"Swish," Tiffany said softly.

Jessica stared at the narrow gap once more. She hadn't climbed under the porch since she was a little girl. It was a dim, cool space filled with garden snakes, old cobwebs, and—at least it was easy to imagine no matter how unlikely—zombie corpses.

She looked around, but there wasn't a single small boy running around the yard that she could send in after it. She gathered her knitting, losing another three stitches in the process, then pulled the three remaining needles out. She snapped the ball of yarn off with a sharp tug and then threw the sock disaster into Aunt Gina's rose bush.

Tiffany looked sympathetic.

Natalya just roared with laughter.

# # #

Greg felt a close kinship to the abominable snowman by the time Dawn and the twins returned from the beach. The sawdust that clogged every pore was brown rather than white—maybe he was more akin to a sasquatch.

They both were.

He and Vincent were coated in a thick layer of wood shavings, sawdust, and a half dozen of the inevitable splinters until their hair, face, and clothes were all of a common oak-dust color. Even the white dust masks looked more like furry Chewbacca muzzles. Vincent tugged his mask down around his neck and tried to hug his wife, who kept him at fingertip distance with a firm hand in the middle of his chest as their lips brushed together.

To balance the scales, Greg pretended he was a goggle-eyed monster and began chasing the twins around the yard with roars on his part and eardrum-shattering giggles on theirs. He finally caught them and gave himself a big shake like a wet dog, completely coating them in sawdust. Soon they were having a sawdust-ball fight with the thick piles that had accumulated under and around the saw. Fistfuls of sawdust flew back and forth—exploding into fine clouds just moments after they were thrown.

One of the twins caught Dawn on the butt.

She turned one of her fierce scowls on the girls and then on Greg. It was enough to cow them all into silence. One of Dawn's strict rules for her husband's furniture making business was: *No Sawdust in the House.*

Ever so calmly, she reached out and gathered a large handful of shavings from the backside of the table saw's fence.

Greg prepared himself for disaster.

Instead, she eased up to Vincent, laying against him and guaranteeing that her front would be coated in dust. She wrapped him into a kiss and just as he leaned in, she rammed her fistful of shavings down the back of his pants eliciting a yelp of surprise.

Dawn jumped back, leaving three moderately clean spots where her breasts and hips had pressed against her husband. Vincent however had other things to concentrate on as he danced and shook his legs trying to shake the itchy shavings out of his pants.

Greg had just started to laugh, when he felt two much smaller hands at his back. They found just enough slack in the back of his own belt to dump fistfuls of sawdust down the back of his own pants.

The twins!

He spun as they rushed away, laughing as high and fast as chickadees.

"Crap! That really itches." In moments he and Vincent were doing similar dances to clear out their underwear. Vincent had already opened his pants, holding them aloft with one hand and digging out the sawdust with the other.

Itching too much to be embarrassed, Greg did the same and began digging great scoops of shavings out of his underwear. How could so much have fit in two such small hands?

He heard a car door slam hard in the opposite driveway.

He turned in time to see Dragon Winslow standing by her car and staring at them. She looked such foul daggers that he was surprised they didn't fall down dead.

Oh perfect.

Then Jessica climbed out of the passenger side and grinned across the street at him.

He tried to close his pants, but instead they slipped out of his fingers. As he reached for them, Dawn gave him a sharp shove. His fallen pants trapped his ankles. Greg fell over sideways and was lost in a puff of sawdust.

Greg decided that he'd just stay here. His best option now was to lie still and wait for the fall rains to come and wash the sawdust and his embarrassment down the ditch and out to sea.

# # #

"That boy, really?" Mrs. Winslow asked Jessica once they were inside, but there was a glimmer in her eye that said it was at least partly a tease.

Jessica looked back out the living room window. Greg and Vincent were both down and now being inundated by the three McCall women. Then Dawn discovered a large garbage bag that must have included previous rounds of sweepings. With the twins' assistance, she dumped it over the two men, then walked off around the house—quickly, a very tactical retreat—waving the girls ahead of her. Probably to hose themselves down in glorious victory.

"That boy, really," Jessica replied, perhaps a little more dreamily than she'd intended. As a matter of fact, it wasn't a reply she'd expected from herself at all.

But she and Mrs. Winslow had sat in the car and watched him playing with the twins. It was clear that the girls loved him. It was also clear what an incredible father he would be. He had a good mind *and* a great heart. Who knew?

"I wouldn't worry, Mrs. Winslow," she turned from the window because she didn't want to keep seeing where her thoughts were going. "I've never found a man worth keeping for long." But if there was one—

She absolutely was not going to be completing that thought.

"Best be calling me Marjorie now or I will have to start calling you Ms. Baxter and we have both been through too much to start that."

"Thanks, Marjorie." It felt wrong on her tongue, but it warmed her through. Mrs. W—Marjorie was like the Judge; her merest presence commanded respect. Being on a first name basis with her after all these years was a mark of approval or acceptance that affected Jessica more deeply than it should for a thirty-two year old worldly woman.

Marjorie led her back into the kitchen. At the end of Tuesday knitting, she'd invited Jessica home for dinner with a simple, "Time we talked a bit and it will be a nice change from eating alone."

Throughout the meal prep she kept Marjorie on the topic of her early years in journalism. She hadn't taken a journalism degree and then simply flown into Saigon to begin filing stories from the front lines as Jessica had always pictured.

"I was working at the *Chicago Tribune*,"—one of the main reasons Jessica had applied to Northwestern University in Chicago and also applied to the *Trib*—"when the son of my editor was killed. She was in such agony, knowing nothing of what happened, that it was tearing her apart. I finally filed for an assignment to go get some hard facts and maybe we would get a couple of good articles out of it. I never found out more about her son, but I spent three years filing from there. Just as in any new job, I began with human interest stories, but things happen fast in a war zone. Soon I was reporting from forward bases and camps."

"But you just came home and stopped," Jessica didn't want to stop. She loved the writing and the connection with readers. She just wanted to be paid for it.

Marjorie Winslow shrugged and set out plates and a bottle of wine with glasses as Jessica set out napkins and silverware to carry out to the back garden.

"Why?"

"Oh, I did another few years. But by that point I was a 'civilian veteran,' if you will. There are things that a twenty-six year old girl born in Portland, Oregon was never supposed to see. I suppose that now it would be diagnosed as PTSD, but all I know was that Chicago—the same Chicago that I had no problem reporting about during the '68 Democratic Convention as a freshman-year student project—felt more and more oppressive until I felt I was being squeezed to death."

Jessica wasn't feeling squeezed. She was feeling…she didn't know what. Her job was to elicit and capture the feelings and experiences of others and interpret that for her readers. She'd done such a thorough job of taking Jessica Baxter out of the equation that even when she did want to know herself, she couldn't find a ready answer.

"My family used to come here for summer vacations," Marjorie continued as if Jessica's psyche wasn't busying thrashing the crap out of her like one of Dad's landed but not-yet-dead fish. "I knew I needed to escape the city, for at least a few weeks. I came here and met Harvey Winslow, local boy retired from the Navy. He was good for me and I for him. We did not talk much, but we understood that talking did not heal things that love and time in a small town could. I never did go back to Chicago; had a friend forward my things."

Jessica slid the two pieces of baked chicken onto the plates as Marjorie added a side of roasted Brussels sprouts. Wild rice completed the dishes and they carried them out back.

It was only then that Jessica realized she'd never been here, never even been in this house before. She was sure of it because there was no possible way to forget the garden.

If Jessica had been asked to speculate beforehand—a practice she'd honed as a journalist so that she was prepared for most eventualities—she'd have expected an orderly vegetable patch, or perhaps a neatly ordered rose garden. Instead, it was an English garden wild in its lushness and lack of conformity. There were trellised roses—though how Marjorie managed that in the harsh coastal climate was hard to imagine. But there were also flowering vines, foxglove past their peak and dahlias just entering theirs, rhododendrons and dozen others. She could see where spring plantings of daffodil, iris, and tulip had died back and where sunflowers were turning to the sun.

"Oh. My. God." Nothing less would suffice.

Marjorie smiled and led her to a small redwood picnic table where they sat. Jessica kept staring about her in wonder.

"I'm in Fairyland."

Marjorie looked about, a calm smile making her look far younger. "This is where I come to play. I missed the lushness of Vietnam's flora, but I also did not want a constant reminder of those times by using tropical plants, even if any would have grown here. This was my compromise and my joy."

Jessica's joy was a fifteen-year-old VW Beetle, battered by its life in Chicago, and one-half of a two bedroom apartment. She'd once had a Ficus plant named Atticus, but it died when she'd forgotten to water it between successive four-week assignments back when she could still afford to have no roommate.

"So, Jessica," Marjorie's tone shifted enough for Jessica to regress right past the twelve-year-old Eagle Cove version of herself into the seven-year-old second-grader sitting at her little desk—her gangly frame already too long to fit properly.

It was that tone that Mrs. Winslow had always used when Jessica wasn't performing up to her potential. Or more typically was busy distracting Natya or Becky because she'd already learned the lesson herself.

"We have heard everything from your mother's short-comings—which she knows full well and does not need *her* daughter reminding her about."

Jessica had already caught herself on that and stopped doing it.

"—To the limitations of Eagle Cove, which those of us who live here know far better than you."

Jessica needed to stop doing that.

"Have you noticed all of the 'For Sale' signs? Or the 'Vacancy' sign on the Sleepy Owl even though it is July?"

She had, but not enough for the implications to really sink in. Some investigative journalist she had become.

"We are too small and remote. People do not even consider visiting here. Cannon Beach, Lincoln City, and Newport are all right on Highway 101 with major feeds over the Coast Range. We are an obscure little town."

Jessica didn't like that at all. The town had always made her a little crazy, but this trip had surprised her at how much she missed it. She certainly didn't want to see it die off like so many of the old lumber towns along the coast.

"But that is all irrelevant to my primary inquiry. Why have you not once mentioned a single thing about your career?"

Crap! She'd been trying desperately to avoid that, but should have known that Marjorie Winslow was a journalist first before she was a teacher. Jessica sawed off a bite of chicken, which was moist and tender so it took no time at all to cut. She stared at a particularly robust sunflower which was peeking over Marjorie's head.

She gave in.

Jessica laid it all out. The successes and the long slide toward impending failure and eventual doom that she hadn't noticed until…well…

"I don't think I understood just how bad it was until I returned to Eagle Cove. Seeing all of these people who I love so much and having no fatted calf to show for my victories. Instead I'm a battered soldier returned upon her Roman shield, except there was no glorious combat to make it an honor."

"Combat is never glorious."

Jessica sighed. She couldn't even get away with a weak metaphor. What was her world coming to?

"But I take your point. Though why you felt that those who love you would think less of you for all of this is beyond me."

"Failure breeds contempt—"

"Is a cliché that is beneath you, Jessica."

Metaphors weak. Clichés failed. What next? Basic grammar? She sawed off another piece of chicken that was tender enough she could have cut it with the edge of her fork. Soon her plate was filled with tiny bits of cut-up chicken, like food prepped to feed a toddler. She dropped her knife and fork on the plate with a clatter as a lost cause.

Lost cause.

She'd say it aloud, but she feared that even analogy was slipping out of her grasp.

"Well, it sounds as if we have a project on our hands this week."

Jessica looked up from her plate to inspect Marjorie Winslow and the sunflower nodding agreement over her head. "We? You can't tell Mom. She has enough going on."

Marjorie dipped her head in consent, "You mother was never the most focused of women."

Jessica poked at her chicken, then managed to eat a Brussels sprout, roasted until it was crunchy-leafed and sweet. "Greg offered to help."

Marjorie looked at her speculatively, "That boy?"

"Yes," Jessica noted the sudden glint in Marjorie's eyes and sighed. "Yes, that boy."

"Man has more sense than I granted him if he managed to unearth before I did what you were hiding so carefully."

"Well," Jessica took confidence from Marjorie's softening expression, "I have spent a lot of time with him these last few days."

"I might have noticed."

"It's almost a pity that I'm leaving in just five days."

"Hmmm," Marjorie Winslow made it a thoughtful sound before returning to her meal.

# # #

Greg had kept an eye out on Mrs. Winslow's house through dinner. He'd thought he was being subtle until Dawn rolled her eyes at him. He shrugged back. How was he supposed to not be distracted by thoughts of Jessica when she was so nearby? Vincent was oblivious of course.

As the evening progressed toward dark and the lights remained off in the house across the street, he finally gave up; he must have missed Jessica's departure.

He was busy losing at some new board game that the twins were ruling through a combination of lucky dice rolls and twin-telepathy—they'd clearly chosen the shared goal of cutting Greg down to size—when Dawn nudged his arm. A light had come on deep in the Winslow residence. Even as he watched, the living room blinked to life and the two women were revealed walking toward the front door: the dauntingly solid Mrs. Winslow and the slender streak of light and air that was Jessica.

If he said goodnight, he didn't recall. He didn't even remember how he came to be waiting at the end of the driveway as Jessica emerged onto the front stoop then turned back to hug Mrs. Winslow. He hadn't known that the old battle-axe was capable of affection, but she held Jessica closely for a much longer moment than mere politeness or even friendship would imply.

Then she looked at him over Jessica's shoulder, because of course the old bat could see in the dark. Her gaze was just as daunting as it had been in second grade. And he still couldn't read what he had done to earn it.

Jessica was most of the way to him before she picked him out of the shadows. She didn't speak or seem surprised. Instead, she walked into his arms, rested her head on his shoulder, and held on tightly. Resting his cheek on her hair, he cradled her and tried to figure out just quite how he'd gotten to heaven.

Back in her doorway, Mrs. Winslow watched them closely for a long moment before closing the door and shutting off the light.

Greg decided that he must be losing his mind because for half a second it looked as if she smiled at him. Not possible.

Now they were shrouded in darkness by the shadows of the late evening and the soft glow of lights from Vincent's windows. Others were awake along Shearwater Lane, but trees separated most properties.

Then the strangest thing happened, Jessica Baxter began to cry. It was soft but there were some things that were difficult to miss with her body pressed hard against his through a thin blouse and slacks. The ripples of gasping breaths down her back, and the warm tears dampening his neck and shirt collar were another sure giveaway. She was the strongest woman he knew, with the possible exception of Mrs. Winslow. Even Dawn had her weak moments.

That Jessica Baxter was crying against him was both startling and oddly enticing. She trusted him enough to cry on his shoulder and it made him feel very strong to be the one she'd chosen to lean upon.

Over the years he'd slowly developed a recipe for dealing with weeping women. In hindsight, it was a little startling how many of them had sought him out when they were sad, but he was thankful for the practice now. He'd learned that trying to stop them only led to harder weeping or, more typically, anger. Instead, he applied a soothing hand slowly rubbed up and down her spine. He had tried the application of a wide variety of meaningless murmurs over the years and had settled on, "Easy now. Easy." And like a good risotto, he just kept his hand moving slowly.

He hoped whatever was making her cry wasn't him. Well, probably not as she'd come to him in order to have her cry.

When she calmed, he gently asked his question, "Is it anything I can help with?" It always earned him a headshake, but it often led to an answer as well. It had even worked on Dawn on the few occasions when she was too frustrated with Vincent to speak to him without bitter words she could never take back.

Jessica, true to form, didn't follow the patterns of other women.

"I thought that you were already working on how to help," her voice was a little rough, but less so than he'd expected.

Help? Help with what? All he could think about was how amazing she felt in his arms and how much he wanted to drag her down on the nearest bit of lawn to…

Oh.

Her career. In tatters. Was that why she'd been in Mrs. Winslow's house? He vaguely remembered that the woman had been a reporter of some sort before coming to Eagle Cove. Something she and Jessica would have in common. Perhaps that had stirred up things.

"I did give it some thought," and had gotten nowhere. But rubbing the tip of his nose through her fine soft hair, he had an idea now.

"Anything useful?" Her voice came out somewhere between a desperate plea and begging as she remained snuggled against him.

"Maybe," he rolled it around on his tongue and liked the way the idea tasted. "Yes, I think so." He breathed her in deeply. There would be some very definite benefits, for both of them.

She waited with held breath, he could feel her diaphragm stop moving.

"You know that I have the money now to open a restaurant."

Jessica nodded uncertainly, then pulled back enough to squint at him in the darkness, only the slightest bit of light from Vincent and Dawn's front window revealing her waiting look.

"I'm thinking that I should open it in Chicago. We can share living expenses and you could help out in the restaurant between jobs. We could—"

One moment she was calmly curled in his arms.

The next moment she was struggling to free herself, shoving hard against his chest to get away.

Greg let her go and took a step back…but there was— nothing there.

He tumbled backward into the roadside ditch. Thankfully it hadn't rained for several days so it was dry and the thick grasses at the bottom cushioned his fall, mostly.

"You are *not* moving to Chicago because of me," Jessica stood at the edge of the ditch, fists on her hips. He was sure that she was glaring down at him.

"Why not?" He leveraged himself up until he was only sitting in the ditch rather than lying in it.

"First, because I won't be a kept woman."

That wasn't what he'd meant, but she continued before he could begin to explain.

"What we have is great—okay maybe better than that—but I'm not shacking up with you here or in Chicago. I thought I'd made it clear that there's no long-term for this girl."

Greg had enjoyed enough short-term flings to know that what was between he and Jessica had nothing to do with those. However, he again recalled Becky's admonition that Jessica would be looking to get away. He decided that pointing out that there was something major between them wouldn't be the best next move.

"Are you okay?"

"Fine. This is a very cozy ditch. I highly recommend it if you are ever out looking for one to sit in."

"Sorry," she moved forward, then stepped back, unsure how to help him up. "I needed a little space, but not that much."

"Sure you don't want to join me?" He assumed not and, clambering to his feet, climbed back up until he was level with her. He shuffled a few respectful steps farther from the ditch.

"Is moving to Chicago to replace my disaster of a career the best idea you've got?" She moved around him, brushing off bits of leaves and dirt.

"So far," he stopped her with a hand and carefully pulled her back into his arms.

She brushed at his chest, but allowed herself to be embraced.

"I'll keep working on it." Then, after placing one foot back to brace himself against another shove, he leaned in to whisper, "but long term still sounds like a grand idea to me."

She growled, but didn't complain or try to get away, when he kissed her.

Chapter 9

Wednesday

What am I supposed to do with him?"

"Why ask me?" Natalya protested. "You're the one getting all of the delicious sex."

Perhaps Jessica should have kept more of the details to herself, despite Natya's hectoring. But the morning run through the forest with her cousin was beautiful and the sex last night with Greg had been delicious. Literally.

She and Greg had been walking home together from Marjorie's when the cool sea fog had slipped ashore. She'd forgotten that the coast was like that. During the summer a few blocks inland could be ten or twenty degrees warmer than the beach itself; at times the line of demarcation was a mere fifty steps wide. Last night it had caught up with them when they turned onto Beach Way. At her shiver, Greg had guided her into the restaurant to grab a couple of jackets. But since they were there…

It had started innocently enough; he'd made her braised pears with a cinnamon-honey glaze and a tiny scoop of impossibly lush vanilla ice cream. A dribble of glaze on her chin had led to a very flavorful kiss which in turn had led to… She'd guessed and been proven right about chefs and kitchens, but chefs and commercial kitchens were a new combination for her and took the experience to a whole other level again. Once he'd peeled off Vincent's "World's Okayest Carpenter" t-shirt—his own clothes were apparently still in Dawn's dryer—Jessica had been as eager as he was to see what trouble they could get into. Her naked chef had quite the imagination and her body was pleasantly sore in so many interesting ways. Some had involved chocolate, others honey, and some just a raw heat that neither of them could seem to sate.

She'd declined spending the night with him; she had too much to think about and he did have a five a.m. start to his day with the Judge. Though they had parted on *very* good terms. Instead of thinking anything, she'd plummeted into a deeply languorous sleep—until Natalya had smacked her awake with a pillow again to go for a run.

"You're not helping," she told Natalya as they both jumped over a thin alder that had fallen across the road. She didn't need a reminder of last night's sex; she needed a solution to, well, everything.

"Wasn't trying to," Natalya admitted happily. This time they were up into the forest and running on logging roads. The night's fog had clung to the beach, but up here in the hills it was significantly warmer despite the trees' shade. The spruce and scrub oak were thick with birds. Stellar jays, so majestic with the black face and crown and bright blue body, dominated. Flickers rattled their beaks against old trees sending echoes through the forest. A red-tailed hawk swooped down through the branches, inspected them a moment, then soared back aloft through a tiny gap in the trees.

"Well try," Jessica did her best to not beg. "That's what cousins and best friends are supposed to do."

"If I'm you're best friend, you must be in more trouble than I thought."

"And don't I know it." Natalya didn't look the least put out by Jessica's jibe. Instead she eased off the pace before replying. They trotted in side-by-side ruts along the road. Thick grass and two-foot-tall alders had taken over the hump between them. It had been years since the last round of logging out here.

"I have advice, but you won't like it."

"Have I ever?"

"Nope. But that doesn't make my advice any less right."

Jessica would feel better if Natalya was a little less on the mark about that in general. "Okay, go ahead. Try me."

"Worry less."

"That's it?" Jessica lengthened her stride to clear a low spot. "Worry less? That's your grand, sage advice that I had to drag out of you?"

"Yep."

"So, I should just give in and enjoy the sex while it lasts."

"Yep."

"And let Greg give up everything that he has going for him here—family, friends, and restaurant—and follow me to Chicago so that he can play Mr. He-man and rescue the helpless waif?"

"Well, no, though he wouldn't be so bad in the role. Besides, since when did you turn into a helpless waif?"

Jessica had no good answer to that one. It didn't sound like her. She'd written lead articles in national publications. She'd won a few regional press awards with hopes of more. The sad thing she'd learned about awards was that the payoffs of winning had been less than the cost of the new dresses to accept the damn things. There'd been no magic rise in her freelancer's fee rates that had fallen out of the sky and into her bank account; no new magazines had appeared begging her to write for them. Actually, it had cost her money in the long run as several of her smaller markets had decided she was too important and expensive for them now that she'd won, even though she'd never hinted at a rate change.

"So, Waif Jessica. What are you going to do now?"

She checked her watch. There was enough time…just.

"I'm going to turn around and beat your ass to the front door of The Puffin Diner and you're going to buy breakfast for two for being such a loser."

"Not a chance."

Jessica opened her mouth to renew her challenge.

Natalya took advantage of the momentary hesitation to shove Jessica sharply off the trail and send her tumbling onto a bed of moss and pine needles. Then Natalya turned and bolted down the hill.

Jessica leapt to her feet and hurried after the hastily retreating figure.

She'd forgotten that Natalya played dirty.

# # #

Greg had his hand on the "Open" sign, ready to turn it to "Closed," when the front door slammed open and sent him sprawling onto the diner floor. The small bell on the back of the door clattered like a fire alarm.

The few remaining diners all jumped in their seats.

Jessica stormed in and started doing a victory dance in the middle of the room. Natalya raced in three steps behind her. Jessica whooped and gasped and danced and gasped some more.

He knew from personal experience that she had splendidly long legs, but lying on the floor looking up at her with her thin runner's shorts and body-hugging Lycra top made them look even longer and more incredible than usual.

Natalya was as scantily clad, a study in dusky skin and powerful curves on a frame as lean as Jessica's. The two of them were dripping with sweat and their morning run had caused their muscles to show more than usual proving that these were two very strong women.

Cal Sr. and a couple of other old timers had been lingering over coffee and the advantage of Cummins versus Detroit diesels for different types of fishing boats and were now all watching the show. Karen Thompson, who had dropped her book with a loud thump and a cry of surprise, was now shaking her head and searching for her page.

"Can I help you?" Greg struggled for some dignity as he sat up on the floor.

"What are you doing down there?" Jessica gasped out and grinned at him, "Again!"

Natalya ignored him and called back to the Judge, "Are you still serving? Please say no."

Greg glanced up at the big clock and knew the answer… they'd cleared the door with fifteen seconds to spare.

"Of course we are," he echoed the Judge.

Natalya cursed, "Crap! She won, so breakfast is on me."

Then Jessica placed her fists on her hips like Wonder Woman and looked down at him. "Are you just going to sit there or are you going to kiss me and show us to our table?"

As he rose he noticed his father's attention was very focused on him. He didn't much care, in fact…

Greg took his time about kissing Jessica. She struggled only briefly, stopping and leaning in even before he could see if she really wanted to escape. He heard the hoots and hollers from Cal's crowd and could feel his father's continued close inspection. Karen he knew would spare them a glance and return to her reading.

When they did finally pull apart, she whispered beneath the on-going applause, "Damn but it's a pity *you* aren't on the menu."

For a kiss like that from Jessica Baxter, every day, he'd put himself on the menu anytime she asked. Price, one golden ring and happy ever after. Her "No way! Never!" stance didn't worry him any longer. At least not as much.

No.

It *didn't* worry him. He knew what he felt and he knew what Jessica felt. And if anyone ever knew what being tenacious meant, it was a chef.

He escorted the two of them to a table and delivered menus with all the finesse of a Michelin-star *maître d'*.

When he reached the kitchen to hand across their order, the Judge had a smile on his face. "You haven't won the case yet, Son, so don't get cocky," he rumbled softly. "But I'd say that you are absolutely on the right track."

He traded a smile with his father and headed back to their table with a small pot of herbal tea and a big mug of hot chocolate with plenty of marshmallows.

Chapter 10

Saturday

Jessica's last few days had gone by impossibly quickly.

She'd spent Thursday afternoon out on the boat with Dad, a glorious day of bright sun, large fish, and happy tourists. The sole damper on the beautiful day was that it was the high season and her father's boat hadn't been full. Those two empty spots had glared at her for the entire trip as if she somehow had the answer.

Money, family, sightseeing, fishing… It was wrapped up in there somewhere, but she still couldn't find it.

Friday afternoon knitting had turned into an extended state of panic for her mother; it was all Jessica could do to keep Monica Baxter distracted from her nerves. Aunt Gina had even abandoned teasing her sister by providing first-night cautionary tales for new brides.

"It's not like you haven't married him before," had turned out to be the most soothing thing to say. Not because it soothed, but rather because it briefly shifted her mother's near panic into a sigh about her own daughter's shortcomings.

Something had shifted for Jessica during her race to the diner with Natalya on Wednesday. It wasn't just that she liked winning, she did. It was a more that she liked the memory of winning but had forgotten what it felt like. Her career had backed her into a corner so slowly that she hadn't noticed until she escaped to Eagle Cove.

And if she wanted to win, she had to get back in the game. The game may have changed, but it was time she took responsibility for her own career.

The afternoons were for Natalya and the rest of her family and the nights were Greg's, but the mornings were hers. Greg had been busy on the wedding prep anyway as the true scale of Monica Baxter's guest list became apparent.

Wednesday after breakfast in The Puffin Diner and then both of the following mornings, after Greg had gone to serve breakfast, she had climbed the steep ladder to the top story of his Victorian house's circular turret.

With the trap door closed behind her, there was just a small couch that was luxurious for one and would be cozy with two, and a circle of windows filled with the most spectacular view imaginable. Beach, water, and sky to the west. The big main house wrapped in trees commanded the view to the south, backdropped by the towering heights of Orca Head and the lighthouse. The sun-dappled forest lay to the east.

She sat there as cozy as a cat in the sun and doodled on a pad of paper. Marjorie Winslow had taught her an appreciation for the blank sheet of paper. She lived with a recorder, a backup recorder, a laptop, a tablet computer, a cell phone... her purse was more about chargers and cables than wallet and makeup. But her favorite tool for thinking was still a pad of lined yellow paper.

Jessica had started with a list of her clients: past, present, and possibilities for the future. The list was a tapering funnel that was going completely the wrong direction, like down the toilet; of course, just when she really didn't want it, the too appropriate metaphor cropped up.

Now recognizing her current career for what it was, and not being fragile—she had to keep reminding herself to purge her secret inner waifishness—she started on building a new plan of attack. She began listing her skill set, then brainstorming alternate markets that she might be able to apply those skills to.

Television news was turning into social media feeds done by the masses which made that industry just as much of a pending disaster area as special-interest journalism.

Intriguing companies, new artists, and innovative thinkers were all doing their own marketing in websites, blogs, newsletters, and again the ubiquitous social media.

Jessica had been a freelancer for so long that she hated the idea of going in and becoming some cog in a corporate marketing department. She'd keep that idea in reserve.

She seriously considered Greg's offer. But it was a senseless. She thought of him without his father, the restaurant, and his friends who greeted him on the streets each morning.

He belonged here, right in Eagle Cove of all crazy ideas. She could finally see that it was true.

By Friday morning, as she sat and watched the tourists wandering the beach, she began sketching Greg's picture in different poses until she found one that she'd liked. Not the naked lover, but the chef serving fine dining. Of the look on his face as the entire restaurant had burst into applause after that amazing halibut dinner. There was a humility there, but there was also a pride. The pride of achieving something long sought after.

There was a catch.

He couldn't run the kind of restaurant he wanted to one or two nights a month. And Eagle Cove didn't have the tourist volume to justify more. It hurt her heart picturing him having to leave this town, leave his home.

Her sketches were starting to form into…she wasn't sure what. She still only had the idea that there was an idea by the time the Friday afternoon knitting session arrived. The sketches were still rough, but she'd thought that the concepts were good even if she wasn't sure yet how they fit together.

She'd showed them to Marjorie anyway.

Marjorie Winslow hadn't said a word. Instead, she'd sent Jessica inside for a glass of ice tea and been gone before Jessica returned. A cautious phone call had elicited no response and no return call. Jessica had hoped that Marjorie would have some piece of sage advice for her career as well, but apparently that was hoping for too much. Now she merely hoped that she hadn't somehow damaged their friendship.

Clearly she'd left so that she didn't have to tell Jessica what she'd really thought of them. That hurt so horribly, that she didn't mention anything to anyone.

She stuffed the drawings and all of her scribblings away, would have torched them if it had been a cooler night and the fireplace had been burning.

Friday night it had been an utterly exhausted man who had collapsed beside her in his bed for a few hours of sleep before he had to return to complete his prep for the Saturday wedding. She had briefly considered showing her ideas to him, but he was too biased—he kept insisting that his move to Chicago somehow made sense—and too exhausted. And she already had Marjorie Winslow's feedback, she certainly didn't need another body slam like that.

Instead, she wrapped around him and held on tight while he slept.

In the morning, they both arose early and parted with little more than a kiss.

She would miss her final private morning in the small tower, but Marjorie's verdict had proved that it wasn't helping anyway. Still, she'd miss it.

Jessica went home. Both of her parents were morning people, so the Baxter household was already on the move by the time she arrived. Dad was in the kitchen making bacon and omelets, Mom was toasting thick slices of Cal Mason Jr.'s slow-fermented sourdough bread. The Blackbird Bakery's sourdough had been built on a starter his father had brought from San Francisco after a stint there in the Coast Guard. Father and now son had been nursing it along ever since and Jessica had never tasted better in any of her travels.

Dad handed over the spatula and whispered, "Keep your mom busy for a minute," then he sauntered out of the room.

Her mother poured her a mug of hot chocolate and leaned back against the counter, "I finally feel calm this morning. It's as if this whole last week hadn't happened."

"Maybe as if the last two years hadn't?"

"Maybe," Mom's smile showed that maybe that was the case. "But I think it was watching you these last few days."

"Me?" Jessica almost dumped the eggs she'd been beating for a third omelet onto the hot stove. "I've been a train wreck these last few days." Damn! She hadn't meant to say that, especially not on the morning of Mom's wedding.

"No. You might have been a train wreck the first few days you arrived here, but something is shifting. I don't know what because you always hold your thoughts so close, dear. I don't even know if it's because of Greg Slater or not. It made you a troublesome child to raise."

"Troublesome?" In hindsight she'd always thought she was too well-behaved as a child. She'd acted out a little as a teen, but she'd been such a good girl that her idea of acting out had been remarkable only in how trivial it was.

"Perhaps troubl*ing* is a better word. You choose; words were always your gift."

As if Jessica was having such luck explaining herself to herself this week.

"We never knew what you were thinking. Someday you'll have a child—"

Jessica bit back on her desire to argue the point.

"You will, honey. And you'll be an amazing mom because you won't be able to help yourself. I just hope for your sake that she doesn't keep her thoughts so carefully hidden."

"It wasn't on purpose, Mom." Only a little. Monica Baxter had always seemed a little frantic and Jessica had never wanted to add to her mother's burdens.

"I know that, dear. Start your omelet. It's just the sort of person you are. Even as a baby in the crib you tended to just watch and think."

She started her omelet and wished she was someone different, but she wasn't exactly sure who. Becky had always been the exuberant one. Natalya had been somewhere in the middle between them. If she herself became any quieter, she'd end up like that girl Tiffany living alone in the woods with her animals, only slipping from her cloister on knitting days.

Jessica poked at the omelet a bit. "You must abuse your omelet," Julia Child said on her cooking show, an episode Dad had made her watch whenever it was rerun. Jessica had never quite had the flare for it, but omelets were his thing. He and Judge Slater often debated omelet technique as if it were a difficult legal case. When it was nearly done, she dribbled some smoked salmon and shredded cheese down the center, then folded it onto a warm plate and slipped it into the oven.

Her father stuck his head back into the room, "Come along you two. I have something to show my girls." Then he was gone again.

"That man," his bride huffed after him. "He can't even sit down to a wedding morning breakfast without starting some project or other. Come along, Jessica. We'll never eat until we admire whatever he's done this time."

They dutifully trooped down the hall, past the master bedroom that would once again hold a married couple tonight… Jessica crossed her fingers on that one so that her thoughts didn't hex it. Past the gym that had been her childhood bedroom and then her father's office.

The breezeway door opened at the end of the hall. There was a lace cloth hanging over something on the wall right beside the door that opened from the breezeway into her mother's wing of the house.

The first thing Jessica noticed was that the stack of notices were gone from the center of the glass door. The taped-down layers of divorce filing, topped by marriage license, topped by divorce filing, and so on—each layer going backward more and more yellow with age—were gone. It took giving her mother a gentle nudge and pointing circumspectly before she noticed the change.

"What are you up to, Ralph Baxter?" Mom's tone was a mix of curious and cautious.

Like a magician, Dad yanked aside the bit of lace.

A large frame hung there. Tasteful, modern, a sea-blue mat around the edges, and nothing in the center of the display.

"That," he pointed a callused finger, "is where our last ever marriage license will be encased tonight for any and all to see. I know it will be the last because my beloved fiancé told me so."

"Oh you," Mom stepped into Dad's arms and held him so tightly. It was a type of hug that Jessica recognized, the embrace of a woman who never wanted to be anywhere else.

An embrace that felt very familiar.

Her father beckoned her forward and soon the three of them were holding onto each other. Jessica didn't cry for a second time, something she hadn't done in years before her episode in Greg's arms, but she came very close.

But this wasn't why her parents' embrace had looked familiar.

Being in Greg Slater's embrace was exactly like what her parents had been doing…and that was the most disconcerting thought of the entire week. If she felt that way in Greg's arms, and Greg truly belonged in Eagle Cove, where the hell did she belong?

That question haunted her for the rest of the morning.

# # #

The midday sun was warm as Greg began unloading his last load of trays into the B&B's kitchen. It felt as if his entire future was riding on this meal, even more than the halibut dinner that had won him his father's financing. He needed the money if he was going to make a splash in a big city, though he wished there was some way to avoid taking it.

But this wedding dinner, a far simpler menu though far more complex in the execution due to the number of diners, was for Jessica's mother. But it wasn't Monica Baxter he was thinking of.

He hadn't even had time to cook one last dinner for Jessica. This evening's post-wedding feast would be tonight's meal and tomorrow morning Natalya would be driving her to the airport.

Dawn pulled him aside on the porch. Vincent had the girls so that Dawn could help him with the prep. Peggy and the Judge would be at the wedding and had both agreed to pitch in with the cooking and service.

"Talk to me, Greg."

"I don't have time for this," he turned back toward the kitchen, but Dawn shifted to stay between him and his goal. He tried to head for the van to unload another big tray of stuffed mushrooms, but she headed him off there as well. What was it with women when he was in a hurry? First Peggy and now…

Realizing that the only way out of this was through it, he dropped onto one of the benches and Dawn sat beside him. She took his hand and held it tightly.

"Shit," was all he could think to say and he couldn't even conjure up much heat behind it.

"There's got to be a way that the two of you can—"

"There isn't! Okay?" He dug his free hand through his hair and barely resisted the urge to start tearing it out. "She's more than I ever dreamed."

"We're not talking pedestal action here, are we? Took me forever to kick out the one Vincent had me on."

"No. It was. But it isn't. Not anymore. I remember, Dawn. I remember when you gave me my first-ever kiss as my fifteenth birthday present and you told me that you were going to marry Vincent so I shouldn't read anything into it. I know that about Jessica Baxter. I know it just as deep as you knew it about Vincent back then."

"Then it's going to happen."

"I don't see how tha—"

"No!" Dawn cut him off sternly. "You listen to me, Greg Slater. If you feel that deeply about her, it's going to happen. Probably in some way that neither of you expect, but it will."

Greg latched onto what hope he could, "You really think so?"

"I *know* so. And remember, I was always the smart one of our group, so you're going to have to trust me on this."

Greg closed his eyes for a long moment, became aware of the warm midday sea breeze brushing over the porch. *Yes. There had to be some way that it was going to happen, so it was time to just believe that.*

He opened his eyes and looked at one of his very closest friends.

"You're the best, Dawn."

"Remind Vincent of that on occasion and we've got a deal."

"Oh, he knows it, but I'll keep reminding him anyway. Besides, I happen to know that you're an amazing kisser and even he isn't dumb enough to walk away from that." He kept it light as that was only one of a thousand reasons his friends belonged together.

"Want to know a secret?" They leaned back on the bench together, holding hands and looking out to sea. For this moment, his need to hurry had sprinted off without him.

"Sure."

"I was scared to death. You were my first-ever kiss too, but I wanted someone to practice on before my first one with Vincent."

"Well, it was great. I still remember it well."

"Want to know another secret?" Dawn's voice was little more than a whisper.

"You're on a roll," he prompted her.

"I've gotten better. Lots better."

Greg could only groan. "Lucky bastard doesn't deserve you."

"Greg?" She asked after such a long pause that his urgent need to hurry had found its way back to him.

"Yeah?"

"I know another great kisser who has probably gotten loads better since his fifteenth birthday. And it is going to be a very lucky girl who gets such a man."

He squeezed her hand hard in thanks. "You might try reminding her of that."

"Nope," Dawn stood, yanked him back to his feet by their linked hands, and led him back toward the kitchen. "You're the one who needs to remind her until she finally realizes how damned lucky she is."

Greg would have to work on that. But at the moment he had a wedding to prepare and cook for.

# # #

Jessica walked down the lawn-green aisle between the admiring crowd as she headed toward her father. It was her, then Aunt Gina, then Monica Baxter, the bride. "Her Mom the Bride." She'd be truly grateful to never have to hear that phrase again as long as she lived.

But for the moment it was just Jessica and her father beneath the sun-dappled coast pines.

For a man in his late fifties, he cut a dashing figure. Strong from the fishing and the projects he was always doing. He'd stayed fit. His best man, Danny McCall looked small and rumpled by comparison.

What would it be like to go walking toward the man waiting for her? Walking on her dad's arm up this same pathway to trade vows with—

Erase! Eradicate! Extirpate!

But her commands to herself didn't work and she glanced aside from the moment she'd been sharing with her father and saw Greg Slater. He hadn't worn a jacket, but he looked just fine in a dress shirt and tie. His collar-length hair, that was such fun to play with, lay tucked back behind his ears. His beard, soft and ticklish, was freshly trimmed short and neat.

He was watching her just as closely with those dark, dark eyes of his. There was no smile, but neither was there a frown. If she had to label his expression, she might be forced to go with "awe." Her bridesmaid dress was a cheerfully frivolous thing that she'd stolen from her mother's closet. Enough of a cleavage for her necklace to lie on bare skin, short sleeves, and a flirty skirt just above the knees.

She passed him by, doing her best to track her eyes forward, but it was hard; far harder than it should be.

The ceremony passed in a blur, as did the meal.

The former a blur of pageantry in true small-town style. There was an equal mix of summer dresses, slacks, and tattered jeans. T-shirts outnumbered blouses or dress shirts and only the wedding party itself was done up to the nines.

The meal was a blur of stunning flavors, succulent dishes, and the mayhem of a hundred people all eating buffet style. The Judge was flipping burgers on a massive grill and Peggy was toasting buns and grilling stuffed mushroom caps close beside him.

In the midst of it all Tiffany slipped up and handed Jessica a small clear food storage bag. Inside was the partially completed gold sock back on its three needles. The dropped stitches had been fixed and the fourth needle lay in the bottom of the bag.

She hugged Tiffany who squawked in surprise, but then hugged Jessica back fiercely before melting away into the crowd. Jessica took it upstairs and tucked it carefully in her carry-on luggage.

Luggage.

She was leaving in the morning.

Jessica sat on the bed a moment and wondered how she could leave. But her life wasn't here no matter how much Greg's was. She'd figured out how to help him, how to help the town a little too.

Or at least she thought she had.

She pulled out the pad with her sketches. She'd develop the idea more this morning, but it wasn't going to pay any bills. It was just an act of—

There was a sentence she wasn't going to be finishing any time soon no matter how true it might be.

The soft knock on the open door behind her had her yelping in surprise.

"Sorry. I should not have bothered you."

Jessica rushed around the foot of the bed and threw her arms around Marjorie Winslow. Marjorie patted her on the back like she was calming an upset child.

"You looked like you were thinking so hard that I almost turned around, but I did not want to climb those stairs again. Getting hard on this old woman."

Jessica held her tighter.

"I suppose that I am glad that I did not."

Jessica was torn between laughter and tears, but managed to go for the former. "You always talk exactly the way you teach second grade, no confusing contractions. I remember you explaining that to me when I asked."

"Third day of class. And you are still the only student I ever had who noticed that I do that."

"It's also probably why you still scare the crap out of Greg and Vincent. I asked, they're both terrified of you."

"Good!" Marjorie turned her and they sat on the bed together. "Keeping those boys on their toes has made them better men. Though Vincent is awfully sweet with his wife and those twins, makes it difficult at times."

Jessica still clutched her yellow pad.

"Those are good, Jessica," Marjorie tapped the pad without looking down. "You have a good eye. You need to give the copy another polish, remember that it is—" she hesitated then enunciated carefully, "*it's* marketing copy not an article."

Jessica nodded. That's exactly what was wrong with it. She flipped through and could see exactly what she needed to do now.

Marjorie made her slow down and they went through the new sketches together.

There were ads for the Judge's breakfasts at The Puffin Diner and Greg's "Evenings at The Puffin." Another spread for her father's fishing trips and her mother's real estate business. Becky Billing's BlueBird Brewery, the Blackbird Bakery… Once she'd started them, she hadn't been able to stop—the pad was half full of advertising ideas featuring the businesses of Eagle Cove. Those had then started turning into ads promoting the coastal town as a destination spot.

"I had a few ideas of my own," Marjorie held out a sealed manila envelope. "Do not—*don't* open it until you're on the plane."

"Okay," Jessica tucked the envelope into the back of the pad and slipped it into her carry-on.

"Now is the time to celebrate a joyous wedding," Marjorie pushed to her feet, brushing off Jessica's attempt to help. "Not that old yet, girl, so do *not* pamper me or I may start to feel that way."

Jessica stayed close beside Marjorie for a long time, their arms linked together in friendship if not support.

# # #

The only way that Greg convinced himself to approach them was already knowing his other option. It was either face Jessica and Dragon Winslow or have Dawn kick his butt for being such a wimp.

Food service was long over except for the two dozen pies he'd made. Cal hadn't had enough warning to make a bigger cake, so Greg had added pies and everyone received a piece of each. He'd made them in all different flavors. He should have made more blueberry, as they were peaking right now on the coast; he'd remember that for next time. Seasonal. Just like his restaurant would be. Yes! He liked that. Whatever was absolutely the freshest.

Dancing had begun. A local band had come together. Vincent's dad Manny sang sweet vocals and Peggy played a mean guitar. Becky had a drum kit and the Judge plucked a stand-up bass. And that odd girl Tiffany was cradling a small Celtic harp. He hadn't even realized she was here.

Greg gave himself one more stern talking to, ignored the inexplicable smile that Tiffany sent his way, and headed for Jessica and the Dragon. There were two very different expressions watching him approach.

Jessica's was everything he hoped for.

The Dragon looked ready to slice, dice, and sear him on the highest heat.

"I'm sorry to interrupt you ladies, but I was hoping for a dance."

"Took you five numbers to talk yourself into that, young man," Mrs. Winslow's tone was accusatory.

"I'm afraid so, Mrs. Winslow." He hadn't thought he was being that obvious.

"Good!" She shared an enigmatic smile with Jessica, untucked Jessica's hand from around her elbow, and held it out to him as if Jessica was a mannequin.

He reached out and took Jessica's hand. The shock of contact rippled up his arm and had his heart skipping.

Without further comment, Dragon Winslow retired from the field of battle and, by some miracle, he still lived.

Jessica slid into his arms, half-time slow dancing despite the band tackling a Doobie Brothers song with some success. She rested her head on his shoulder and wrapped her arms around his neck.

"She likes you, you know."

"That'll be the day. I can't stand that you're leaving tomorrow."

Jessica tensed in his arms, definitely the wrong thing to say.

"How about," he tried again, "we just dance and let tomorrow take care of itself?" It must have been the right thing to say, because she slowly relaxed once more until there was nothing but her in his arms and somewhere, seemingly far away, the sound of music and laughter.

Late in the night, as they lay together in his bed not wanting to sleep and miss a moment before the dawn light, she whispered to him.

"You can't follow me, Greg. Please. It's the one thing I ask of you, don't follow me."

"Will you come back?"

The silence stretched forever.

"I'll try."

For now that would have to be good enough. What he wasn't going to tell her was that if she didn't return soon, he was damn well going to follow despite her order. And he had the sneaking suspicion that almost everyone would be on his side with that decision, perhaps even Dragon Winslow.

He spent the rest of the time before dawn doing his best to make this a night she couldn't forget even if she wanted to. And he knew for a fact that she didn't want to, she just didn't know it yet.

Chapter 11

A Week Sunday

*T*he ads had started appearing on that first Wednesday after she was gone. They slipped out into social media channels.

By Thursday the town had a promotional website. It was slickly functional but friendly and welcoming.

By Friday it was the talk of the morning breakfast crowd, the only talk.

Greg was as stumped as everyone else, almost everyone else. The Judge was in on whatever was happening, Greg was sure of it, but he refused to be pinned down.

The reviews hit on Friday, a week after Jessica's departure. Write-ups appeared in *The Oregonian*, the Newport *News Times*, and even the *Seattle Times*. The bakery in one, Ralph Baxter's fishing trips in another, and reviews of both of the meals that he'd cooked while Jessica was visiting.

He knew she had to be behind it. The initial ads had sounded like her, but with a very different flair. It wasn't until the reviews came out that he knew for certain. Those were definitely in her prose style; that powerful writing voice he'd so appreciated in her early days.

The big splash hit on Sunday.

"Puffin Days at Eagle Cove!"

There was a roster of events.

Puffin boat tours!

A special weekend opening of the Puffin Diner, along with the Judge's menu.

Brewery tours.

And right in the middle of every ad, a massive announcement of the opening of "Evenings at The Puffin." Gourmet food Friday and Saturday nights only.

He'd finally confronted the Judge with it over Sunday dinner in the big house.

"Well, that is interesting," his father had inspected the ad at leisure. "I suppose you had better start planning a menu. You have a restaurant to open."

"No! I have a woman to go see. I was going to fly to Chicago next weekend and track Jessica Baxter down whether she wants me to or not."

The Judge just nodded sagely. "Guess that you know more about opening a restaurant than I do, but it looks to me as if you're setting up to disappoint a potentially large clientele."

The Judge slid across a reservation sheet. Across the top it said "Evenings at The Puffin." Beneath that were columns of names. Two seatings on both nights. It was already a packed house.

Damn it! Jessica was just trying to make sure he didn't leave Eagle Cove. It would help if it wasn't the perfect solution to almost everything. He already had the restaurant and a local group of patrons. They couldn't sustain him for a full restaurant opening, but they could certainly provide a solid base for his launch. With everything that would be in place, including his living expenses, he wouldn't need a cent of his father's money. His savings would cover it all. Hell, with four sold-out seatings he might be adding to his bankroll rather than depleting it.

It was perfect except for the lack of Jessica Baxter in his life. But she'd trapped him and she knew it; he couldn't leave.

"You thought much about a ring when you do finally see her?"

Greg startled. If his father thought he needed a ring, then maybe, just maybe there was a way this could work.

"I was hoping that getting on my knees and begging would be sufficient. I figure Jessica is the sort of woman who would want to choose the ring herself."

"Still got a lot to learn about women, Son." His father reached into a pocket and pulled out a small box. His expression was tight and unreadable as he slid it across the table with just his fingertips.

Greg opened the box carefully…and knew right away there was no better ring to be found.

The two stones were the emerald green of the forests and the blue sapphire of the sea. The forest and the sea met here in Eagle Cove as they met nowhere else.

It was his mother's ring.

He stood and walked around the table. For the first time since her funeral, Greg hugged his father and just held on as the Judge patted him on the back.

Chapter 12

And One Week More

*J*essica's *VW Beetle made* it over Maxine Pass without too many complaints. It had been a hard three-day drive from Chicago, crossing the endless expanse of the Great Plains, through the heart of the Colorado, Wyoming and Utah Rockies before turning northwest into Oregon. But she could practically coast from here.

The car felt as if it knew the way. Somewhere in the last two weeks since Mom's wedding the control of her future had slipped out of her hands—or at least any future she had recognized.

She'd slept for most of the flight back from Portland to Chicago, only remembering Marjorie Winslow's envelope an hour before landing at O'Hare. There were only a half dozen pages; the first page was a hand-written letter on lined yellow paper:

My dearest Jessica,

I could not be more proud of you if you were my own daughter. You have achieved so much. And you did it while staying true to your heart and your ideals. That is a truly rare achievement.

The market has changed out from beneath you, now it is time for you to be brave and change with it.

Know that whatever you decide after reading the enclosed, you could never disappoint me.

I love you very much.

Marjorie

Jessica had cried for a second time in as many decades, right there in seat 24E.

What she felt as she read through the rest of the envelope's contents was neither sadness nor joy—it was wonder.

The Coast Range stream that had run beside her mother's car just three weeks ago, once again raced her down through the trees. The Doobie Brothers song that she and Greg had danced to played over the car's stereo.

The contents of the envelope revealed why Marjorie Winslow had rushed away from the Friday knitting group. She'd approached the town's merchants. They had all, each and every one, chipped in to finance a contract. Mom's Eaglet Real Estate had been first on the list and her father's Eaglet Fishing and Charter had been next. It wasn't much, at least not in the first year—though there was a very respectable bonus structure if her efforts were successful.

It was a contract for Jessica. The merchants of Eagle Cove wanted her to entice tourists to their town.

The final sheet had been one of Marjorie's sheets of yellow paper. Unlike the friendly letter, it was concise and to the point. So concise that there were only two words inscribed on the entire page:

Think festivals!

It had been a vote of absolute confidence that with that two-word hint she would know what to do.

And she did.

Every skill she had learned as a freelance journalist responsible for making her own career translated perfectly into marketing a town like Eagle Cove.

"Puffin Days" was the first festival—a starter test case for her future concepts. It was also the best she could do on two weeks' notice. If all of her efforts had worked, it should be in full swing by now.

Nerves shivered up her body. In another dozen miles she'd know. And if it did, Puffin Days would become the recurring anchor point of the summer season. In her file, resting on the Beetle's passenger seat, were sketches for fall, winter, and spring events.

She slipped into town and couldn't find parking anywhere— the place was packed. Her nerves kept climbing. Not even the salty sea and the mossy forest could calm her.

Jessica found a space out by Marjorie's house and left the car. It was enough of a signal for her friend to know that she'd made it into town. It was packed with all of her worldly belongings—everything that hadn't fit in the tiny car, she'd sold or given away. Not quite "the clothes on her back," but close. She should knock and say hello, but she couldn't be delayed.

She walked into town, tracing the path toward The Puffin that a very different woman had walked a mere two-and-a-half weeks ago holding hands with Greg Slater after knocking him into a dry ditch. Exactly as planned, it was just at the start of the Saturday dinner service. Her mother and father had made a reservation for three without explaining why to Greg.

So many things now made sense that never had before.

She didn't feel twelve at all.

Jessica felt like a grown woman.

And there were choices that a grown woman could make. As much as she loved her mother, Jessica knew that she was different. Once she'd made her choice it would be forever.

It was finally as clear as the summer sky just turning orange above the crowded and busy streets of Eagle Cove. As clear as the bright sound of the bell on the back of The Puffin's door.

Tonight, either she or Greg was going to go down on bended knee.

And tomorrow the rest of their lives would begin.

Together.

About the Author

M. L. Buchman has over 40 novels in print. His military romantic suspense books have been named Barnes & Noble and NPR "Top 5 of the Year," nominated for the Reviewer's Choice Award for "Top 10 Romantic Suspense of 2014" by RT Book Reviews, and twice Booklist "Top 10 of the Year" placing two of his titles on their "The 101 Best Romance Novels of the Last 10 Years." In addition to romance, he also writes thrillers, fantasy, and science fiction.

In among his career as a corporate project manager he has: rebuilt and single-handed a fifty-foot sailboat, both flown and jumped out of airplanes, designed and built two houses, and bicycled solo around the world.

He is now making his living as a full-time writer on the Oregon Coast with his beloved wife. He is constantly amazed at what you can do with a degree in Geophysics. You may keep up with his writing by subscribing to his newsletter at www.mlbuchman.com.

Coming soon, Eagle Cove #2:

Recipe for Eagle Cove
(excerpt)

An air of delighted mischief pervaded the B&B room as Becky and Natalya changed out of their bridesmaids dresses. Jessica Baxter had always sworn she would never marry and instead she was the first of the three friends to go down…and they were going to make her pay for being so fortunate.

Becky peered out the second-story window; it was easy to pick Jessica out of the crowd which spread across the broad lawn. The stately Victorian stood well back from the high bluff above the rolling Pacific. The bride was down on the lawn below: long, blond, sleek, and gorgeous in white lace. The afternoon sun of the warm September day—because *of course* it wouldn't dare rain on Jessica's wedding—sparkled off her as if she was half elf and half fairy. Both of which Becky had always suspected to be true.

And Becky couldn't begrudge one of her best friends getting Greg Slater because the two were so perfect together. But she could be envious. And the only proper way to deal with envy was merry revenge.

She couldn't suppress her giggle as they were changing. Natalya flashed a grin back at her; Jessica's first cousin was like the anti-Jessica. The two of them were both tall and thin, but Natalya was dusky-skinned, brunette, and had curves that Jessica had whined about not having since forever. It had been Natalya's idea for them to change into little black dresses for the wedding reception, as if they were mourning Jessica's demise. Half pixie, which were always a tricky lot, Natya was the strategist of their childhood trio.

Becky had been the one to fashion matching corsages for them out of black tissue paper. Those eighteen years of schooling had finally paid off, even if it was just in crafts projects from the First Grade. She preferred the down and dirty of the last fourteen years since graduating from Puffin High.

She turned back to the room and saw that she had another problem. Natalya in a little black dress was going to knock out every man around and Becky didn't think that was much more fair than Jessica looking so ridiculously happy.

Becky looked in the mirror, not that it did her much good. Natalya lived three hours away in Portland, so was staying in the Writer's Room of her mother's Victorian B&B. It was an airy, lofty-ceilinged room typical of the old architecture. This room was filled with books, images of writers, and the décor was pure Jane Austen-era Georgian. That meant that the mirror had a massively ornate, gold-painted frame. Despite its imposing presence, it was actually small, round, and set far too high for Becky's five-four. That her two best friends since kindergarten were both five-ten was just another cruelty. What she'd lacked in stature she'd made up for in curves, "lush Italianate curves" her similarly shaped mother had always said—which made perfect sense with their pioneer-stock, Gold-Rush era, boringly Anglo-Saxon heritage. Not!

She was… Becky had never been able to pin down what she was. Imp? Garden gnome? The right metaphor always eluded her.

Unable to see her reflection much below the generous cleavage that even the most conservative little black dress gave a woman of her shape—and this dress was not meant to be conservative—she turned to Natalya for help.

"Your mom's stupid mirrors. Help me, Natya!" It was an old problem that didn't need explaining.

Natalya whirled a finger and Becky did a turn on the ornate Persian rug that looked as if it had been snatched out of the Hogwarts Gryffindor Common Room, making the room all warm and cozy. J. K. Rowling watched Becky from her portrait over Natalya's shoulder. Emily Dickinson considered one profile and Jane Austen the other. Maya Angelou may have been inspecting her shoes. She'd pulled on her bright red cowboy boots with the pretty black stitching. The low heel was good because of dancing on the lawn and Becky's conviction that high heels on a short woman were just a lame form of sucking up. And whatever James Tiptree, Jr. was thinking about Becky's shoulder-length auburn hair, she was keeping to herself, just as she'd kept her gender hidden through two decades of writing science fiction.

Natalya shot out a thumbs up. "Men are going to whimper!"

"Yes!" Becky offered a fist pump and did a little circular stomp dance on the rug. "That is if they notice me with you around."

"Since when have you ever had to worry about that?"

"Since Jessica looks so damn happy dancing with Greg." Together they turned to look back out the window. Becky half wanted to collect the writers' pictures from the walls so that all of the women in the room could look out together.

"It *is* a little like she's bragging, isn't it?"

Becky could only nod. Jessica was draped shamelessly against her new husband, slow dancing to an up-tempo Backstreet Boys song. Three months ago Jessica had come back to Eagle Cove after a decade working as a Chicago journalist. She was supposed to be here just a week and then return to her whirlwind urban career. Instead, she'd stayed as the town's new marketing manager and was kicking ass at it. Tourism was at its highest level in five years, or maybe twenty-five. That was good news for the Lamont's B&B, Jessica's mom's real estate business, and it certainly hadn't hurt Becky's brewery.

"Time to go break up all of this unmitigated happiness." It was. And Jessica was right, Natalya was always the sneaky one of the group.

"First dibs on cutting in on the bride for a dance with the groom," Becky declared just as Natalya was opening her mouth to do the same.

"Damn!" Natalya's curse warmed Becky's heart.

To secure her victory, she raced for the door, offered an air high-five to Nora Roberts' picture, and beat Natalya to the stairs. But she was blockaded from escape at the bottom of the stairs…the kitchen was packed. She was in the midst of the fray, when across the impenetrable mob, she saw Natalya slink down the old servants' back stairs and out onto the porch. Her wicked grin showed exactly where she was headed—to claim the second dance from the groom.

"Damn!" All she could do was echo Natalya's heartfelt curse of a moment before. Becky stomped her foot in frustration; growing up in this house gave Natalya an unfair advantage.

#

Harry yelped more in surprise than pain as someone tromped on his toes. The kitchen was so noisy with a dozen simultaneous conversations that no one particularly noticed his cry. It took him a moment to spot his attacker, but when he looked down he discovered an astonishing sight.

The first thing he noticed was the impressive swell of exposed breasts. It wasn't that they were all that uncovered, they were just very…impressive. *Ah yes, his lawyerly finesse with words. Sad.* But it was hard to be completely coherent when faced with such an exceptional view. Then he forced himself to focus on the owner's face.

"Becky!" He ignored her smirk that said she knew exactly where his attention had first landed and gave her quick hug that she returned after a moment. "It's like old home week." Everyone had turned out for his little brother's wedding. The fact that Greggie was marrying, *had* married, the first woman Harry had ever kissed didn't bother him…too much. He and Jess had been almost done before they started during freshman year. Wasn't it a lark that Greg was the one who'd always had the big crush on her without ever admitting to it.

"Old home week only to you foreign types." The smirk had shifted to tease, something he recalled Becky Billings excelling at.

"Foreign as in a hundred yards down the road." His family's homestead was the other grand Victorian of the town. The two old houses stood at the head of the beach and commanded the best views in Eagle Cove.

"Foreign as in you live in New Orleans and are just here slumming."

"Care to do a little slumming with me?"

"You call that a pickup line?" Becky snorted out a laugh and slapped him hard enough on the arm to send him ricocheting off Cal Mason Jr. who bumped into Cal Mason Sr. in earnest conversation with Jessica's father. Cal Sr. shoved Jr. back into him and the two of them ended up tangled together against the stove, both struggling not to spill their beers all over each other.

"Sorry, Cal, Becky just—" he pointed, but the spot where she'd been was empty. Cal gave him a look as if checking his mental capacity: low, after the view of Becky's chest had drained the blood out of his brain.

He looked around and caught occasional glimpses of the top of her head as she moved through the tight-packed kitchen crowd, her liquid-oak hair floating lightly behind her. The crowd parted just enough to offer him a full view as she stepped out the far door and onto the sunlit porch.

She might be short, barely up to his chin, but her industrial-grade curves and trim waist looked damn good on her. And that dress. Spaghetti shoulder straps, clinging material, and a flirty flare high enough on her thighs to reveal that she worked for a living. She was no runner, couldn't be with that body, but they were damned amazing legs. Then with a exuberant "Yip!" of excited greeting, loud enough that he could hear over the music and the dozens of conversations, she raced out into the sunlight and was gone.

Harry rubbed his shoulder where she'd hit him. He'd forgotten how strong she was. He'd have to remember that the next time he caught up with her. And the way she looked, he definitely had some catching up to do. But he didn't want to look overeager either. So, he leaned back against the stove with Cal. They'd been the two forwards on the soccer team back at Puffin High, finishing the season ten-and-two, a new pinnacle for the Pufflings. Cal Sr. and his own father, Judge Slater, had chosen the ridiculous little seabird as the school mascot half a century before. He'd never found out quite why, so he and Cal Jr. worked on their beers and rehashed it some for old times sake.

But what he really wanted to talk about was Becky Billings and the way that woman looked in a clinging black dress with chili-pepper-red cowboy boots.

Available soon at fine retailers everywhere

Other works by M. L. Buchman:

Angelo's Hearth
Where Dreams are Born
Where Dreams Reside
Maria's Christmas Table
Where Dreams Unfold
Where Dreams Are Written

The Night Stalkers
The Night Is Mine
I Own the Dawn
Daniel's Christmas
Wait Until Dark
Frank's Independence Day
Peter's Christmas
Take Over at Midnight
Light Up the Night
Christmas at Steel Beach
Bring On the Dusk
Target of the Heart
Target Lock on Love
Christmas at Peleliu Cove
Zachary's Christmas
By Break of Day

Firehawks
Pure Heat
Wildfire at Dawn
Full Blaze
Wildfire at Larch Creek
Wildfire on the Skagit
Hot Point
Flash of Fire

Delta Force
Target Engaged

Deities Anonymous
Cookbook from Hell: Reheated
Saviors 101

Thrillers
Swap Out!
One Chef!
Two Chef!

SF/F Titles
Nara
Monk's Maze